Grave Robber

Lynne Sella

WingSpan Press

Printed in the United States of America
Published by WingSpan Press, Livermore, CA
www.wingspanpress.com
The WingSpan name, logo and colophon are the
trademarks of WingSpan Publishing.

First Edition 2010
ISBN 978-1-59594-417-7

Library of Congress Control Number: 2010932822

This book is dedicated in loving memory to
Ron Asher
February 15, 1940 — December 31, 2007.
Thanks for believing in me.

ACKNOWLEDGMENTS

First I would like to thank my family and friends for their patience during the writing of this novel. I would especially like to thank Mike and Lindee Larson for introducing me to Surprise Valley and for giving Deputy Sarah a place to live. I also owe thanks to the experts in law enforcement who responded to my emails and willingly answered my numerous questions. Chip Jackson, retired Emergency Services Chief for Lassen County provided me with procedures and common practices for the deputies employed there and shared some of his personal experiences. Stacy Callaghan, a member of the Drug Task Force and one of the many deputies to have patrolled Surprise Valley, imparted his experience with and knowledge of the Modoc County Sheriff's Department. A special thanks to Ron Asher, retired Special Agent of the Federal Bureau of Investigation for his insight and experience in the FBI. Last but not least, a big thanks to all my readers who have been subjected to numerous rewrites and who have given me invaluable feedback. I couldn't have done this without you.

Chapter 1

"It'll be easy. Practically nobody knows about this place. Just box the stuff up and wait."

The old man takes another sip of his whiskey. "When did they say they'd be back?"

"Some time next spring. We'll have plenty of time to dig."

"What's this 'we' business? Sounds like I'm the one doing all the work."

The taller man runs his fingers along the scar on his face. "I told you why I ain't digging. Besides, I can't get away from work without somebody asking a lot of questions. Are you in or not?"

The old man empties his glass and slams it down on the table. "What the hell, I'm in."

The front door exploded into a thousand wooden splinters before my ears registered the sputter of automatic weapons' fire. Agent Sloan bailed off the porch in one direction and I went the other. Pulling my Sig 9 mm out of its holster, I rolled into a crouching position and, in spite of the freezing cold, slipped out of my long coat. "That was too close for comfort, wasn't it?" When I got no answer, I fumbled through the coat's pockets for my MagLite and crawled through the crusty snow.

"Are you hit?" I rolled the man over and clicked on my flashlight. The snow where he had lain was crimson.

Before I could see how badly he'd been hurt, another volley of gunshots erupted from the back of the house. "Shit!"

I dropped the light, grabbed my cell phone and hit the pre-programmed button for 911. After identifying myself, I gave my location and requested assistance from the local authorities and an ambulance. As I slipped the phone back into my pocket, another short burst of gunfire was followed by a much louder single shot that I assumed was Hensley's .357 Magnum.

"He's down!" Special Agent Morgan sounded close by.

"Over here," I called, holstering my weapon. I recovered my MagLite and pulled back Sloan's blood-drenched shirt. He'd been hit in the chest. When I applied pressure, he moaned and his eyes fluttered open. "Hang on, Randy. Help's on its way." He gave me a weak smile and closed his eyes again. Why hadn't Hensley listened to me?

We'd been parked along the dark street for about forty minutes. It was so cold the dusting of snow that had fallen a few days earlier still lingered on the ground. The frigid air seeping into the vehicle chilled my feet and pushed out any heat that remained. Pulling my wool coat tighter around me, I wiped the moisture from the window and peered out at the quiet neighborhood. "Are you sure this is the place?" I blew on my hands to warm them.

"According to the tip we received, Amir Schmidt lives at the end of this cul-de-sac. Personally, I think we're wasting our time." Special Agent in Charge, Richard Hensley took off his glasses and cleaned them on the end of his tie. "Not to mention, freezing our asses off."

"No kidding. Why would a world-class arms dealer be living in the outskirts of Leesburg, Virginia?" Agent Randall Sloan had just finished his training at Quantico and was assigned to our Security Unit. He and Special Agent Morgan were hunkered down in the back seat.

"That's right, rookie. I'm thinking the same thing, and if nothing happens in the next few minutes, I say we call it a night. What do you say, Morgan?" Hensley replaced his glasses and settled further into his seat.

"Suits me." John Morgan, a.k.a. Hensley's Henchman, never strung together more than a few words at a time. He'd followed Hensley up through the ranks, and in my seven years as an FBI agent, I'd never seen him anywhere other than just behind Hensley's right shoulder.

As we sat in silence trying to stay warm, a dark Buick sedan cruised past us and pulled into a driveway three houses away. A short, stocky man climbed out and went into the brick building. Minutes passed but the house remained dark.

"Why isn't that guy turning on any lights?" Agent Sloan asked. "That's just plain weird."

"Probably has blackout shades over the windows. Let's go pay him a visit." Hensley opened his door.

Still not seeing any indications that someone was inside, I reached out and touched his arm. "This may sound kind of corny, but I've got a bad feeling about this."

"Oh really, Murdock. Is that your woman's intuition or are you PMSing again?"

My face flushed, and I gritted my teeth. "I think we need more agents than just the four of us. This guy is dangerous."

"Were you able to make a positive ID of the man?"

"It was too dark, but he fits the general description," I offered.

"So does my Uncle Vinnie. I still think this is a case of mistaken identity, so let's go check it out. Then we can all go back to our nice warm homes. Come on." Hensley exited the black SUV, followed by Sloan and Morgan. I'd gotten out too, feeling that the whole thing was a mistake. And now Agent Sloan was lying in the snow, possibly bleeding to death.

"Just as I thought — piece of cake." Hensley and Morgan came around the corner of the house.

"You call this a piece of cake?" I yelled at him.

"What the hell happened?" Hensley knelt down on the other side of Agent Sloan.

"He got hit when that maniac opened up on us."

"Damn it! Morgan, get an ambulance."

"I already called for one, but I've got to stop this bleeding. Get the first-aid kit out of the car."

Hensley stood and nodded at Morgan. Then he retrieved my coat and draped it over my shoulders, but it didn't help. I continued to shake.

By the time Morgan returned with the first-aid kit, I could hear the wail of the approaching sirens. With trembling, bloodstained fingers, I tore open a handful of gauze bandages and pressed them into the wound. Agent Sloan opened his eyes again. "Sarah?"

"Don't talk. The ambulance will be here soon." Less than a minute later, it pulled into the dead-end street, followed by several local police cars. The paramedics bailed out, grabbed their gear, and pushed their way into position. They plucked Agent Sloan out of the snow, placed him on the gurney, and began working on him.

I backed out of the way and watched as uniformed officers climbed out of their cruisers and began milling about. Some guy in a cheap suit hooked up with Hensley, and the two of them disappeared around the side of the house.

The blood on my hands began to dry, making the skin on my fingers tighten and pull. I tried washing them in the snow, but it didn't do much good; I looked like the survivor of some B-rated horror movie. When I realized I was still shivering, I slid my arms into the sleeves of my coat and started toward the SUV.

One of the paramedics, a short thin man in his late thirties, left Agent Sloan's side and stepped in front of me. "Hang on a second and let me check you out."

"No need, I'm not hurt. Just a little cold is all."

"Then that's not your blood?" He nodded toward the top of my head.

Running my fingers along my hairline, I felt a gash in

my forehead and a patch of dried blood but there was no pain. "Is it bad?"

"It may need a stitch or two; otherwise it might leave a scar."

"Just what I need — another scar."

He led me over to the front steps and had me sit down. Then he pulled out his penlight and got a better look. "How did this happen?"

"No idea. Must have been wood from the door."

"Could be. At any rate you need to have that looked at."

"Now?" Surely there was something I should be doing, although I couldn't think what it might be.

"Why not? You can ride in with your friend there." Again he nodded, but this time it was toward the ambulance where his partner, with an officer's help, was loading Agent Sloan.

It only took about two seconds to decide. I'd much rather make the long trip to the hospital with the paramedics than Hensley and his goon. The man could really be an asshole; I just wished I'd figured that out before I'd slept with him.

"Whatta you mean you're taking time off? You haven't had a vacation in five years." Sue James added a packet of sweetener to her tea and stirred it. Then she popped the lid off her deli salad, picked out the packet of dressing and threw it away. Such sacrifices had to be made to maintain her size 5 body.

"Don't give me a hard time. I just need to get away for a while." I leaned against the pockmarked counter, waiting for my lunch to finish heating in the microwave. The puce-colored walls and scuffed linoleum of the small room on the fourth floor of the Bureau were not conducive for a lingering lunch. Most of the agents either grabbed something at the deli around the corner or ate at their desks. Sue and I, however, preferred the dismal little room and frequently had lunch there together.

"So how's the kid doing, anyway?" She pierced a few lettuce leaves with her fork and placed the small bite in her mouth with skilled precision.

"He's one lucky rookie. It was just fragments from a bullet that caught him. Only broke a rib, but he's not the reason I need a break. It's Hensley."

"What did the jerk do now?"

The timer dinged, and I pulled my red-hot bean and cheese burrito out of the microwave, juggling it back and forth until I could plunk it onto a paper plate. No size 5 for me. "Let's just say he's using our previous relationship, however brief it was, to persuade me into his way of thinking."

"I still don't know what you ever saw in that guy." Sue and I had met our first day at Quantico and had connected immediately, even though we had almost nothing in common. She'd tried to tell me I was making a mistake, but I didn't listen.

"Can we not go there, please? I was young, anxious to get started on my career as an FBI agent. When Hensley told me I had potential, I thought he meant with the Bureau."

"So what's he want?"

I tore open the plastic wrapper, slid the burrito onto the plate and cut it in half. "More like what he doesn't want. He doesn't want me to include the misgivings I had about the whole thing in my report."

"You mean he wants you to lie?"

"Not exactly. Just leave out anything that might make it look bad for him."

"I take it back. He's not a jerk; he's a rotten bastid!" Sue thrust her fork repeatedly into her salad until she had a huge bite. Then she shoved the whole thing into her mouth. After chewing furiously, she continued. "I say we stake him out over a hill of red fire ants."

Being an eighth Apache, Sue was very proud of her

Native American heritage. In fact, it was her desire to protect those treasures and traditions that brought her to the Art Crime Team unit of the FBI. Her straight black hair and bronze skin gave her an exotic look, which was a sharp contrast to her Bostonian accent. And when angry, her brown eyes blazed and she always had some heinous torture in mind. A true friend.

"Maybe you should just stand up to Hensley. Tell him to piss off and write the report your way."

"I'd love to but I don't think I can trust him. So far he's been quiet about our little indiscretion." I finished off my lunch and threw the trash away. "If I cross him, now that he's my supervisor, it could mean the end of my career."

"But he was a willing participant. How could he do that?"

"Believe me, if there's a way, he'll find it. I just don't want to take that chance."

"How long are you going to be gone?"

"At least until after Christmas. I thought I'd go home for a while. Mom's been bugging me to come back to California for the holidays." I stepped over to the vending machine and decided on a Three Musketeers bar.

"You mean you're gonna miss the ski trip up north?"

"Yeah, but that's all right. I'm not that great of a skier. Always afraid some tree's going to step out in front of me."

"Oh you're just so wicked funny. Not. When do you leave?"

"Next Friday. That'll give me time to do some shopping. Which reminds me, I need a favor."

Sue ate the last of her salad and snapped the lid back onto the empty container. "For you, anything. As long as it doesn't involve Hensley."

"Don't worry, it doesn't. I just want you to check on Raven a few times while I'm gone. Maybe take him a carrot or two."

"You spend too much time with that horse. Why don't you put that much effort into your relationships?"

"The horse I can relate to. The men, on the other hand..." Before we could continue our discussion of my love life, Hensley strode into the room.

"You got that report done, Murdock?"

"Not yet, but you should have it by the end of the day."

"See to it that I do." Without another word, he spun on his heel and left.

Sue slammed her salad container into the trashcan. "Fucka!"

Chapter 2

The flight west was uneventful, thanks to good weather and traveling before the holiday rush. Within thirty minutes of landing at Sacramento International Airport, I had my luggage in the trunk of my rental car and was zipping up Interstate 5, bound for Red Bluff.

It felt odd to be surrounded by the spaciousness of California's central valley, unlike the perpetual urbanism of the east coast. Even so, the valley was not as vast as before; housing developments and strip malls seemed to be swallowing up the last of the farmland once and for all.

Further north, new orchards crowded the freeway instead, their tiny trunks still smooth with youth. I vaguely recalled some conversation I'd had with my dad on the phone. "Almonds, the new cash crop of California."

Nearing Williams I needed a break, so I pulled off the freeway and drove to my favorite deli. Or at least to where it used to be. A huge pile of rubble had taken its place. Swinging into the mini-mart across the street, I settled for a polish dog with extra relish and a diet soda.

"What happened to Granzella's?" I asked the cashier. The guy was over six feet tall and looked to be of retirement age. His balding head was wreathed with gray hair, and his prominent belly led me to believe he sampled his own wares frequently.

"Burnt down last summer. Made a hell of a bonfire too. Folks could see the black smoke for miles."

"They going to rebuild?"

9

"Rumor has it they're putting up a more modern building with two drive-ups, one for the deli and one for the market. Drive-thru olives, imagine that."

"Yeah, imagine that." I carried my food to the car and sat looking at the remnants of the local landmark. Granzella's old-fashioned meat counter had held all the ingredients for the best deli sandwiches for miles. The little market sold all kinds of goods produced locally as well as its own selection of olives, which customers dipped out of open barrels. The bar was a favorite hangout for locals and the small restaurant rarely had an open table.

I wondered if the place would be as inviting with its new building, or would it end up like most other places, where tourists were herded through as they made their way up and down the interstate. As I pulled back onto the freeway, I understood for the first time the saying, "You can never go home."

It was late afternoon by the time I pulled into my parents' driveway, the place where I grew up looking smaller yet newer than I remembered. The old cracked planking that my sister and I were required to paint every five years or so had been replaced with pale yellow, vinyl siding. An aluminum roof, the same color red as the crisscross brick sidewalk, had taken the place of the moss-covered cedar shakes. The long rectangular piece of lawn — mowed with a near antique human-powered lawnmower that my father referred to as a character builder — was now an undulating carpet of green with a decorative stream running through the center of it. Strategically placed saplings and an occasional boulder provided the finishing touches to the small piece of acreage any golf course would have been proud to call its own.

As I climbed out of the rented Pontiac Grand Prix Sedan, my mother burst out the front door, her five-foot-four frame practically twitching with each step. "Sarah, I'm so glad you're home. We've missed you so much." She all but knocked me over throwing her arms around me. "Your father has been so excited about you coming home."

Maybe, but I highly doubted it. Frank Murdock didn't get excited about much. After working for the California Department of Forestry for fifty years — he never could get used to its newfangled name, CAL FIRE — he'd had his share of emergencies. And being a no-nonsense, take-charge kind of guy, he had met each one head-on. No panic, no emotion, just deal with the situation and wait for the next one. So to say that my father was excited may have been an exaggeration. My mother Lela, on the other hand, had such an enthusiasm for life; it was hard to keep her feet on the ground.

"Where is Dad, anyway?" I stepped to the back of the car and opened the trunk.

"Oh, he's finishing up one of his projects with his new tractor. You should see it; it's a cute little green one."

Somehow I didn't think my dad would appreciate having his farm equipment referred to as cute. I pulled out my khaki canvas bag and slammed the lid back down.

"Is that all you have? Well, come on. I have your room already for you. We just finished making it over into an office for me. I volunteer for so many organizations these days, the paperwork got to be more than the end of the dining table could handle."

I followed my mother up onto the front porch, which had also been redone, right down to the green indoor/outdoor carpeting. "Looks like you guys have been busy," I said as we make our way into the house.

"Mostly your father. He can't stand being idle. Always has to have some project he's working on. Right now he's building a duck pond at the back of the property. That way the birds will come to him." I plopped my bag down next to the couch. "You don't mean he intends to sit out there and shoo—?"

"Heavens no! Frank traded his shotgun for a camera

a few years ago. He says it gives him the same kind of thrill and he doesn't have to clean the darn things."

I thought about our early morning hunting trips to the canal, lying in the freezing cold muck, waiting for the ducks or geese to fly by. As if reading my mind my mother continued. "He won't have to get up before daylight either. Says the best light for taking pictures is around midday."

I could just imagine my father sitting in his favorite lounger, the camera strap around his neck, an ice chest of beer on one side, his faithful hunting dog on the other, waiting for the ducks to land among his decoys. No wonder he gave up hunting.

"Come on, let's get you settled." My mom reached down and took hold of the straps, but my bag didn't budge. "What on earth have you got in this thing?"

"Here, I'll take it." I picked up the bag and followed her down the hallway. The room I'd shared with my sister looked completely different. The twin beds had been replaced with a large computer desk on one side and a small, white enamel daybed on the other. The small dresser had been joined by a four-drawer filing cabinet and an overflowing bookshelf.

"The top drawer is empty, and there's room in the closet. Get unpacked and as soon as your father gets cleaned up, we'll go out for dinner."

More proof that things never stay the same. Lela Murdock would have never taken guests out to dinner. A cook at the local high school for thirty-five years, she prided herself, or used to, on being able to throw together a meal to remember. As I put my things away, I held onto the hope that there'd be biscuits and gravy for breakfast in the morning. Funny what makes you feel like home.

When I was done, I wandered back out to the living room, but no one was there. Looking through the large plate-glass window, I spotted my dad driving his "cute" tractor back toward the house. My mother stood waiting for him, hands on her hips, at the edge of the lawn. I let myself out the back door and joined her. As he got closer, I started laughing. Duke, his golden lab, was perched on what looked like a custom-built platform.

"You must have spotted your father's copilot," my mom said. Together we watched the pair climb down off the tractor and stroll toward us.

"I see you have lots of help," I called to my dad.

"Yeah, ol' Duke and me..." Before he could finish, a raucous gobbling sound erupted behind me. I spun around into a right back stance and threw my hands up into a square block. A large bird with an ugly bluish-white head atop a long red neck stood where I had been. Its brown and black feathers had white stripes running through them.

My dad started chuckling. "That's some fancy footwork, Sis. Don't believe I've ever seen you move that fast. What do you call that move?"

Heat rose up my neck and into my face. "Oh it's just a self-defense pose I picked up in my Tae Kwon Do class." My muscles relaxed and I straightened up. "What is that, a wild turkey?"

"Isn't he just the sweetest thing?" My mom bent down and rubbed the turkey's chest. The large bird opened his wings, flapped them, and let loose another gobble.

"Follows your mother around like a damn dog."

"Where'd you get it?"

"His name is Lucky, and we found him while we were hiking in the woods. Looked like he'd wandered too far from his nest and gotten lost. Your father scooped him up in his ball cap and we brought him home. At first we kept him in a small coop but soon discovered he liked to follow us around. Even Duke tolerates him; they curl up together on the back porch for their afternoon nap. Now, let's get ready and go have some dinner. How about Casa de Ramos?"

"Sounds great and we can go in my car," I offered. There was probably more room in Mom's Ford Taurus station wagon, but the way my parents drove made me crazy. Lela's constant chatter tended to pull her attention away from the road. Frank, on the other hand, had a top speed of forty-five regardless of the posted speed limit. It was just easier for me to drive.

A little while later, we were sitting in a cozy booth at our favorite Mexican restaurant north of Red Bluff. The tortilla chips were warm, fresh out of the fryer, and the salsa had just enough heat. "How's Lydia doing these days?" I asked, hoping the waitress would return soon with my beer.

"Uh, Lydia — well she..." My mom glanced at my dad.

"What? Is there something wrong?"

"Not exactly. It's just that Alexis — I mean Lydia..."

"Who's Alexis, and what does she have to do with Lydia?" Hundreds of thoughts raced through my mind, none of them good.

"Well, you see..."

"Oh for Pete's sake Lela, just tell the girl."

"Tell me what." The waitress returned and set our drinks on the table. I had a couple of big swallows while I waited.

"If you remember, your sister got that wonderful job as a buyer for Nordstrom's..."

"Yeah."

"Well, she felt the name Lydia wasn't sophisticated enough and..."

"It was certainly good enough for my mother." My dad took a long draw on his own beer.

"Now, Frank this has nothing to do with your mother." Turning back to me she continued. "So she changed her name to Alexis."

"I see." But I didn't. I never really understood anything my younger sister did. She and I were so different it was hard to believe we had the same parents. "So is Lydia — I mean Alexis — coming for Christmas?"

"Well, actually..." At that moment our food arrived, and when my mom didn't go on, I prodded.

"So is she?"

"Is who what?"

"Lydia."

"Alexis," my mom corrected.

"Whatever! Is she coming for Christmas?"

She didn't answer right away. Instead, she proceeded to spoon salsa over her taco salad, which came nestled in an enormous flour tortilla shell. Finally, when she'd emptied the small brown bowl of salsa, she spoke. "No, she's spending the holidays with Sterling and his family."

Who the hell is Sterling? I looked to my dad, who was halfway through his platter of "La Favorita," for answers. Sensing my curiosity, he paused just long enough to mutter, "Boyfriend."

"Actually he's more of a fiancé," my mom added.

Good grief. Even when my sister wasn't around she was annoying.

"Which brings me to the question..."

Here it comes!

"...when are you getting married?" Lela Murdock has been asking her daughters that question for about ten years. And until now our answers had always been the same. "We're not ready yet." But apparently one of us had changed her mind.

"Now, Lela don't badger the girl. She just got here."

"What about that young man from the FBI? Hinckley, was it?"

I practically choked on my chicken enchilada. "Hensley, Mom. His name is Richard Hensley, and we haven't been together for at least a year." I emptied my beer and looked for our waitress. Not seeing her, I got to my feet. "I need another one. How about you, Dad?"

"Sounds good."

I zigzagged around the tables and found a place at the bar. "Two Coronas, please." I dug a ten-dollar bill out of my pocket.

"Man, they'll let anybody in here."

Recognizing the voice behind me, I turned around and found myself face to face with an old high school friend. "Hi, Scott." I slid off the barstool, reached up and gave him a hug. "This is a nice surprise."

"Hey, Sarah. I haven't seen you since our tenth reunion. Are you here for the holiday?"

I nodded as I reclaimed my perch. "Mom's been bugging me for a while now to come home for Christmas."

"Still giving the terrorists hell?" He flashed his crooked smile at me as he settled on a barstool of his own. Aside from the crow's feet developing at the corners of his green eyes, Scott Jenkins looked pretty much the same as he did when we were seniors.

"Oh yeah. Knocking them off right and left." The fiasco in Leesburg popped into my head, and I shuddered. "What about you?" Before he could answer, the beers arrived.

"You planning on drinking both of those?"

There's a thought. "Here, have one on me." I pushed a bottle toward him. He plucked the lime off the top and chugged the beer. "You still working at the mill?" I asked, squeezing lime juice into my own.

"Nope. It's been closed for a couple of years. I'm a deputy sheriff for Modoc County now."

A giggle escaped before I could stop it. "You're a deputy?"

"What's so funny?" The smile melted from his face.

"Oh, I'm sorry. It's not that I find it funny, it's just hard to believe that you're now the person we avoided most of our senior year, what with all the under-age drinking."

His smile reappeared. "Yeah, I know what you mean. Who would've guessed?"

"So what's the life of a deputy in Modoc County like?"

"Not nearly as exciting as being an FBI agent, I'm sure. Other than Alturas, the county hasn't changed much at all. It's still mostly one-horse towns and sprawling ranches."

"Unlike the central valley, huh?"

"You ain't kidding. I can't believe how different it is here now. Nothing like when we were riding the rodeo in high school."

The rodeo. I hadn't thought about that for a long time. Scott, his two brothers, and I hauling our horses from one fairground to another. We'd been all over northern California competing, occasionally winning a scholarship or two. "You still ride?"

"Oh sure. I go to a roping every now and then, but mostly I ride for pleasure these days. I have a little place just outside of Alturas. Nothing big, just a few acres for the horses to run around on."

"How many you got?"

"Right now I have three. Sport, my roping horse, a two-year-old Arabian I'm working with, and Fancy."

"Fancy! That old mare is still alive?"

Scott laughed. "Sure is. Too ornery to die I guess. She still rules the roost too. Keeps the other two in line. How about you?"

"I got into endurance riding on the east coast. Found me a nice thoroughbred gelding that I board at a small stable in Stafford, Virginia. Other than that, most of my time is spent working."

"Boy I wouldn't mind seeing the kind of action I'm sure you're used to. About the only time we get any is when the highway patrol has a high-speed chase coming through. Otherwise, we spend our time patrolling, maybe break up a fight at a local bar or help roundup wayward livestock. Some of the deputies, the real hard-core ones, can't stand it, so they either move where there's a higher crime rate or try another line of law enforcement. In fact, Sheriff Chet Atkins..." Scott's eyebrows rose and he grinned at me. "Get it, Chet Atkins?"

"Get what?"

He shook his head. "Never mind. Anyway, the sheriff has a position he'll need to fill in a couple of months."

"Really? Do you think..."

"There you are. I had the waitress save your dinner." My mom held up a large Styrofoam box.

Scott stood and nodded toward my parents. "Mr. and Mrs. Murdock."

"Oh look, Frank. It's that nice Jenkins boy. Steven isn't it?"

"Scott, ma'am. Scott Jenkins."

"Oh yes, of course."

I rolled my eyes and gave Scott a quick shrug of my shoulders. He winked back. "Hey, maybe we can get together. I'll be at my folks' until the twenty-sixth.

"Sounds good. See you later."

"That's such a nice young man," my mom said as we maneuvered toward the front door. "I never did understand why you and he..."

"Come on, Mom. We were just friends in school. I mean, it would've been like dating my brother."

Chapter 3

The savory smell of sausage and toasted biscuits wafted into the room. Thoughts of creamy, white gravy and the aroma of fresh-brewed coffee were enough to get me out from under the warm covers. Still on Eastern Standard Time, I'd been awake for a while, enjoying the rare luxury of lying in bed and thinking about my conversation with Scott.

I was beginning to question the save-the-world-from-the-terrorist thing, and the mess with Hensley still bugged me. I'd sold myself out, and for what? There was no guarantee that he wouldn't hold the whole thing over my head again in the future. Anybody else would have had the decency to keep it to himself, but not Hensley. That's how he'd advanced so quickly in the Bureau. Get the dirt on someone and then threaten to reveal all if he didn't get his way. He was a real piece of work, as Sue would say.

I rolled out of bed, added a pair of sweats to the oversized Green Bay Packer T-shirt I used as a nightgown, and ran a comb through my hair. Not glamorous but good enough for breakfast with the family.

"Well, look who's up before the chickens." My dad was in his usual spot at the kitchen table reading the paper.

I grabbed a cup and filled it with steaming hot coffee. The digital clock on the coffeemaker read 5:30. "What are you guys doing up so early? I thought you were supposed to be retired."

"Old habits die hard and besides, this is the best time of the day."

Good grief. Frank Murdock has turned into a walking cliché.

"One biscuit or two?" Mom asked, stirring milk into the pan of gravy. Beneath it sat a brand new stove, which matched the new dishwasher and huge side-by-side refrigerator/freezer. The worn Dutch-style linoleum resembling miniature brickwork had been replaced by hardwood flooring.

"Two please, with extra gravy." I made a mental note to somehow burn it off later. "So, what's on the agenda for today?"

"The women's auxiliary is putting together a craft show this weekend and I'm co-chairman, so I'll be gone most of the day." She placed a heaping plate in front of me. The sight and smell of the food made my mouth water. I picked up my fork, cut off a large bite of biscuit, lifted it to my mouth and then stopped.

"Is there something wrong?" my mom asked.

"No," I said, staring at the cake-like piece of biscuit dripping with gravy. But what if there was something wrong? What if it didn't taste the same? What if it had changed like everything else?

Suddenly I felt like I was in the Twilight Zone. I'd come home to rest and get a reality check, but this wasn't reality; it wasn't the home I remembered. What if...

WHOA! Get a grip!

Closing my eyes, I placed the bite in my mouth with the same precision I'd seen Sue James use hundreds of times. The bite melted, sending the flavor of butter and sage everywhere. It didn't taste the same; it was better than I...

Huh? My eyes popped open to discover my dad staring right at me. "Did you say something?" I asked around what remained of the heavenly bite.

"I said, I'm sure I have an extra shovel you can use if you want to hang out with me today."

"Thanks for the offer Dad, but I think I'll pass." I took another bite, savoring it like a culinary delicacy.

He chuckled. "Thought you might."

"Actually I have some shopping to do, and I might try to hook up with some old friends," I said after swallowing.

The conversation waned as we finished breakfast. I offered to clean up the kitchen, which got my parents out of the house and gave me time to plan my day. I decided to give a Scott a call and learn more about the opening in Modoc County. The rest of the day I'd spend looking for presents. Christmas was less than a week away, and I hadn't bought a thing.

By ten o'clock I was dressed in my black pantsuit and heading north on Interstate 5. I'd called Scott, but he was off somewhere with his brother. I explained what I needed to Mrs. Jenkins, and she gave me the number of the sheriff's office in Alturas. After being on hold for several minutes, Sheriff Atkins agreed to meet with me but only today; he was leaving first thing in the morning for a much-needed vacation.

Just past Redding, I turned west and began the climb into the surrounding mountains. As I negotiated the twists and turns Highway 299 made through the tall pine trees, I considered my options. I could stay in Washington D.C. and kiss Hensley's ass, but that would make me as inept as John Morgan. Requesting a transfer was another alternative, but I'd probably have to relocate. That could prove difficult with Raven, and I wasn't ready to give up that part of my life. The only other choice was to leave the FBI and start a new career. At least that way I decided where to live and wouldn't have to worry about Hensley any more. Perhaps running into Scott was the twist of fate I needed.

Three hours later I arrived at the sheriff's office in downtown Alturas. The single-story building had a flat roof and was surrounded by sprawling juniper bushes. The rough brick walls were unbroken by windows except in the front. Two large sheets of glass flanked the front door, allowing personnel inside to observe anyone that approached. A much larger facility stood behind it, which included a high wall constructed of concrete block topped with razor wire.

As I entered the building, I heard the receptionist speaking to someone over the radio. The name placard on the tall, circular counter that surrounded her desk identified her as Cindy Evans, Dispatcher.

"I'm Sarah Murdock," I said, when I got close enough to see her. "I have an appointment to see Sheriff Atkins."

"You must be the one who called earlier." A voice crackled from the radio behind her. "Hold on a sec." She spun her chair, picked up the mike, and responded. "Copy 120. Time is 13:28." She replaced the microphone and stepped around the desk. "I expect him back any minute, so you can wait in his office. Right this way." I followed her down the hallway and into the second room on the right. "Make yourself comfortable." She pointed to the two chairs in front of the sheriff's desk and left.

Settling into the seat closest to the door, I looked around trying to get a feel for the man. The top of the desk was uncluttered; a black desk set organized paperclips, note pads, pencils, and pens. A large blotter, with stacks of files on either side, took up most of the flat surface. A credenza attached to one side provided space for his laptop. Photographs of horses rather than people hung on the walls, and a small round table with matching chairs crowded the corner behind me. A low bookcase filled with several thick books sat by itself along one wall.

I was beginning to have second thoughts about being there when the sheriff walked in. He was not a big man but walked with the confidence of someone much taller. His curly brown hair was clipped close to his head, and his uniform was immaculate. He sat at his desk and began flipping through files, looking for something. "Let me see, you are..." He continued to hunt until he found a small piece of green paper. "Sarah Murdock," he read.

"Yes sir, that's right."

"Well, Ms. Murdock..." He replaced the paper, laced his fingers together and rested his arms on his desk. "... what can I do for you?"

"I understand you're looking for a new deputy."

"How did you find out there was going to be an opening? I haven't placed an ad in the paper yet."

"I ran into Deputy Jenkins in Red Bluff. He's an old classmate."

"Jenkins. Good man but not nearly as funny as he thinks he is."

"Yes, sir. We kind of felt that way about him in school."

"What kind of law enforcement experience do you have?" He drew a yellow legal pad out from under one of the stacks, pulled a pen out of its holder, and began to scribble.

"I've been an FBI agent for the last seven years, assigned to a security unit in Washington D.C."

"The FBI?"

"That's right."

"And now you want to do something else?"

"I haven't really decided yet." I shifted in my chair. "Just exploring some different options."

"I see. Well, let me tell you what you'd be getting yourself into here. Each deputy has his..." he paused "... or her area to patrol. They handle anything that might come up but request backup if the situation is more than one deputy can handle. The new deputy will be patrolling Surprise Valley."

"Isn't that where Cedarville is?"

"Are you familiar with that part of the county?"

"I used to ride in the rodeo at the county fair."

"Yeah, they do pack them in for that every summer. Anyway, most of my deputies don't care to patrol Surprise Valley. About the only thing that happens over there is an occasional rowdy night at the bar or a missing prize bull."

"I understand."

"Mind you, it's not an easy job. Lots of territory to

cover, which means hours and hours spent in the vehicle."

Alone with no one to complicate my life.

"My deputy is leaving the end of February. If you're interested, you'd need to go through a few weeks of orientation to get familiar with our procedures and regulations. And of course, you'll need time to find a place to live. I can give you the name of a realtor in Cedarville. If there's a place available, Liz Leerman will find it." Sheriff Atkins pulled a pink business card out of his desk drawer and handed it to me. "You'd be taking over, say the end of March."

"That would give me plenty of time to hand in my resignation and wrap up the investigations I've got going." *And take care of some unfinished business.*

"So, are you interested in the job?"

"To be honest, I'm not entirely sure."

"Well, I still have to advertise and take applications for the position, but based on the kind of applicants I've had in the past, I'd say you're definitely qualified." The sheriff stood and walked around his desk. "Why don't you fill out an application on your way out and leave it with Cindy. That way I'll have your contact information and we'll be in touch."

"Sure, not a problem." I shook his hand. "Thanks again for your time."

A little while later, I was sitting in a hamburger joint on the edge of town, eating a double bacon-cheeseburger and looking at the realtor's card Sheriff Atkins had given me. Seven years was a long time to just walk away, but as I weighed the pros and cons of staying versus leaving, I had to admit that remaining with the Bureau could be a huge mistake. Finally I decided to give myself a few days to think it over, but first I had to survive Christmas with my parents.

Chapter 4

"I had no choice, I tell you. The guy walked right up behind me while I was unloading the car. Threatened to rat me out if I didn't cut him in." The old man rubs his bristled chin.

"Well keep me out of it." The taller man moves to the next cage and tosses in some lettuce and a few carrots.

"Too late for that. He knows you're in on it 'cause he told me he heard us talking about it at the Silver Spur."

Even though the morning commute into Washington D.C. had ended at least an hour ago, traffic on Interstate 270 inched along bumper to bumper. Every time my lane began to move, some idiot pulled in, cutting me off. I'd slammed on the brakes so many times I was sure Raven was scrambling to stay on his feet.

My head pounded and my mouth was dry. I'd flown back to Virginia to hire a moving van for my belongings as well as pick up my horse and drive him west, and Sue had invited me to spend the night at her place. We stayed up until well past midnight visiting and drinking most of a twelve pack. The last time we'd done that was the night I told her I'd applied for the job as deputy sheriff.

"You can't be serious," she'd said, her brown eyes burning right through me. "Don't tell me this thing with

Hensley is going to make you throw away the past seven years."

"I'm very serious, and Hensley isn't making me do anything."

Sue went into the kitchen and returned with a couple of ice-cold beers. "So what's your folks think about this?" she asked, handing me one.

I popped the top and took a drink. "My dad thinks I'm making a mistake because of my retirement. Mom's excited because I'll be closer to home. The way I look at it, things happen for a reason, and maybe my job here is done."

"Whatta you mean your job is done? How can it be done? I mean, there are terrorist threats every day that..."

"Sue!" I raised my hands in surrender. "Let's not get excited. I may not even get the job." But I did, and when I handed in my resignation, Hensley was furious. He stuck me riding a desk and gave all my ongoing investigations to Randy Sloan. If Hensley had known how much easier that made it for me to leave, he'd have never done it. Taking me out of the field also provided me with the perfect opportunity to submit an amended report about Leesburg, which I had turned in on my last day with the Bureau.

Nearing Hagerstown, the cause of the traffic jam came into view. A small delivery truck had tangled with a semi, rolled, and strewn its payload of computer components all over the freeway. Road crews had managed to clear a path, which was being used to funnel all three lanes of traffic past the chaos. I was grateful when the road opened up again, and I could put some space between me and the other vehicles.

Crossing into Pennsylvania and onto I-76, signs warned me of the upcoming toll. As I began to gear down, I fumbled in my pocket for the change left over from the two bear claws and large orange juice I'd purchased before leaving Stafford. Dropping it into the cup holder of the console next to me, I counted out three dollars and sixty-five cents; I was thirty-five cents short of the toll. There was more money in my wallet but nothing smaller than a twenty. I eased into line and began frantically searching for coins. Inside the console I found a dime and two nickels cowering under my CDs. I still needed fifteen cents. Feeling the pocket of my jeans one more time, I realized there was still a coin inside. I said a small prayer, reached in and pulled out a quarter. *Saved!* Without even counting out the exact amount, I tossed the whole handful of money into the collection basket and drove on, happy to make the small donation to the Pennsylvania Department of Transportation.

Just before reaching Pittsburgh, I caught I-70, heading west. My original route, compliments of MapQuest, had me continuing on the turnpike until it merged with I-80 somewhere around Cleveland. I altered my course for two reasons, an additional thirteen dollars in tolls and sleeping in a horse trailer within fifty miles of Lake Michigan in March. That could be cold, especially when my only heat source was a very small electric heater.

Needing a place to sleep during my endurance competitions, I'd converted the trailer's dressing room into a cozy sleeping area, complete with a cot, refrigerator, miniature microwave, adjustable shelving, and a porta-potty for emergencies. Wired for 110, all I had to do was pull into the nearest KOA campground, plug in, and I was set. Driving cross-country towing a horse trailer, I had decided to do the same thing, and my first stop was a KOA just outside of Dayton.

Around one o'clock, I reached Wheeling, West Virginia. The pastries I'd wolfed down for breakfast while waiting for the movers to load my things out of storage were sitting in my stomach like a couple of bricks, so I opted for a salad and a bottle of water at the first McDonalds I passed. I'd just finished my meal and was strolling out the door when Raven started kicking the inside of the trailer.

"I hear you, boy," I said as I walked past his window.

"We've got a ways to go yet, so just simmer down." I crawled up into the front seat and fired up my Ford Dooley.

After making the decision to compete, I'd purchased the horse trailer and a diesel truck to pull it. Fortunately, I rode the Virginia Railway Express into Washington D.C. every day and didn't have to negotiate city traffic in the massive vehicle. And living in the same apartment complex as Sue, we'd often ride somewhere together in her Toyota Camry.

Continuing west on I-70 we made good time, and I hoped to be in Dayton by five o'clock. Just as the sun sank low enough to interfere with visibility, I spotted the large yellow KOA sign and instructions to take the next exit. Feeling stiff and tired, I gratefully moved to the right and headed off the freeway. I followed the arrows, but as I approached the entrance I realized the gate was closed; the sign on it read, "Open April 1 - November 1." I was twelve days too early.

How could I have missed that small detail? In all the times I'd stayed in KOA campgrounds, I never ran across one that had been closed. Then it dawned on me; all my competitions had been between April and November. I pulled the directory out of the glove compartment and looked for the nearest open KOA. There was one in Wapakoneta, but that was fifty miles out of the way to the north. The one in Indianapolis had supposedly opened the first of March, but when I called on my cell phone to make sure, the woman who answered told me they were full because of some race at the Speedway. My only other choice was to drive across Indiana to Terre Haute. I called the number for that campground and was assured that they were open, had plenty of room, and would be expecting me. Not looking forward to the additional time on the road, I turned around and eased back onto the Interstate.

When I finally reached Terre Haute, I was exhausted. Thirteen hours on the road had taken its toll on me as well as my equine companion, who was rapping his front hooves against the steel of the trailer. The sun had disappeared a couple of hours ago, and I still had to put together the makeshift corral for Raven.

I pulled through the gate of the KOA and stopped in front of the office, which was not hard to miss. The small chalet-like building looked like the miniature IHOP I used to frequent with my family, and my stomach instinctively growled. I'd just started up the short walkway when a man stepped out the front door.

"You must be the gal that called earlier." He was just under six feet tall, and his dark blond hair, which brushed the collar of his plaid shirt, was unkempt and laced with gray. He strolled toward me, his hands shoved deep into the pockets of his denim overalls.

"Yes I am and..."

Raven began banging around inside the trailer again.

"Sounds like your passenger is getting a little anxious."

"He's not the most patient horse I've had."

"You're not going to leave him in there overnight are you?"

"Oh, no. I have panels to make him a small corral."

"I'm sorry young lady, but that won't do." The man shook his head and scratched his face through his short, shaggy beard.

"Let me assure you, sir, that I'll leave my space exactly as I found it. We've stayed in KOAs all over, and I've never had any complaints."

"That's not what I mean. You look plain tuckered out and I'm sure your friend here is too. I've got a paddock over yonder where we keep our Mini Ds and you're welcome to use it for the night."

"Mini Ds?"

"Miniature donkeys. We have three of the little fellas, but they sleep in the barn at night."

"Thanks, Mr. ..."

"Name's Everett."

"Everett, that's very generous of you."

"Glad to do it. Let's get your horse unloaded and I'll walk him over while you park your rig."

I opened up the back of the trailer, slid over the panels, and released the interior divider. When I patted Raven on the rump, he practically exploded out of the trailer. "Maybe I should walk him around a bit first," I said, grabbing his halter as he shot past me and snapping a lead rope onto it.

"Don't you worry none, Miss. Before retiring and settling in here, I used to handle racing stock much more spirited that this here fella. We'll manage just fine." He took Raven's lead rope and guided him toward the small barn and its adjacent pen. "You can have this spot over here," he said, pointing to a space nearby.

I closed up the horse trailer and backed it in next to the small barn. After hooking up the 110, I switched on my fridge, plugged in the space heater, grabbed my big flashlight, and went to check on Raven. He was munching contentedly on a flake of hay that had been tossed out for him.

"Well, you sure lucked out, didn't you boy?" I said, reaching over the fence and scratching him between his ears. "I'll be back in a little while with your blanket and some oats."

Anxious to get settled in for the night myself, I walked back to the office and stepped inside. "Thanks again for your help." I reached into my wallet for my credit card.

"Always glad to help out a fellow horse-lover. What time you planning on pulling out in the morning?"

"I hope to be on the road by six."

"I don't turn the Mini Ds out until eight o'clock; you're welcome to stay until then if you like. Besides you won't want to miss out on breakfast. Homemade muffins and waffles hot off the iron."

"I have to be in California by Thursday afternoon to

meet the moving van, so I better be on my way sooner than that."

"Suit yourself. Just something to keep in mind if you decide to sleep in."

"Thanks, I'll do that. Good night." I had only two things on my mind before going to sleep. First I needed a hot shower, and then I had to double-check the list of campgrounds where I planned to stay.

After getting Raven's blanket in place and giving him a double-handful of oats, I grabbed my stuff and headed for the showers. The hot water beat between my shoulder blades, slowly easing the stiffness in my back. Unfortunately, it also zapped the rest of my energy, and by the time I got back to the trailer, I could hardly keep my eyes open.

I pulled a burrito out of the fridge and popped it into the microwave. While it heated, I grabbed the KOA directory out of the truck and sat cross-legged on my cot. Checking the three campgrounds I'd chosen, I was relieved to discover they all were open year-round. Coming as far as Terre Haute had also shortened the next day from ten hours to seven, so I decided to take Everett up on his offer, sleep a little longer in the morning and have breakfast before pulling out. Hopeful that the worst of the journey was over, I ate my meager dinner and went to bed.

The next morning my stiffness was back. Moving slower than usual, I grabbed a change of clothes and stepped out into the cool, crisp dawn. A light frost covered the grass and coated the fencing of the corral as well as Raven's blanket. Redbud trees in full bloom shot bursts of deep pink throughout the surrounding, bare-twigged trees. I hurried toward the bathroom, anxious to get the day started.

By the time I'd secured my things in the trailer, my muscles had loosened up, and my stomach was demanding food. The complimentary continental breakfast was in full swing when I got there. Fellow campers filed past a counter where large, clear containers of dry cereal were flanked by a bowl of fresh fruit and a tower of muffins. A small crowd hovered around the dual waffle iron, anxiously awaiting the crispy, golden disks. Forty minutes later, I'd eaten my fill, loaded Raven into the trailer, and was continuing on my way west.

The drive across Illinois was uneventful; the weather was clear, and the traffic was light. But shortly after crossing into Missouri, conditions changed. Large black clouds began forming to the west, and strong winds buffeted the vehicles. Just as I reached the outskirts of Wentzville, a warning sign flashed its lights and directed drivers to tune-in to a frequency on the upper range of the AM band. The pre-recorded voice informed me of a high wind warning and possible thunderstorms developing along the western border of the 'Show Me' state. A few miles further, torrential rain and dark skies forced me to reduce speed.

Reaching my destination by mid-afternoon, I parked in front of the office, which was an exact replica of the one in Terre Haute, and dashed inside. The registration desk was on one end of the room and a marginal convenience store took up the rest.

"Welcome to Kansas City." The short blond standing behind the counter looked like she'd just stepped out of a beauty salon. Her nametag identified her as Alice Boudreau, owner. She pushed a registration card toward me. "Are you a KOA member?"

"Sure am," I said, pulling out my wallet. "I'll only be staying one night. We're on our way west."

"How many in your party?"

"Just me."

"But you said 'we'." Our conversation had attracted the attention of a small group of people milling about the shelves of the convenience store.

"Oh, I'm moving my horse to California."

"Horse?" Any and all other action ceased; all eyes were on us.

"Yeah, he's out in the trailer."

"Well..." She glanced at the others. "It's staying in the trailer isn't it?"

"Oh no, I have panels to make a small corral."

"You can't..." A huge clap of thunder made everyone jump.

"That sounded close," I said, offering her a smile. Others in the store nodded in agreement.

"Yes, too close. Spring storms can be very unpredictable. Now, about your horse..." She shook her head.

"Mrs. Boudreau, Raven is very well-behaved, and you won't even know we've been here. I promise."

"Well, I don't know..." Another clap of thunder helped her decide. "Fine, park in space 36." She slapped a diagram of the campground down onto the counter in front of me. "It's toward the back and should be out of the way," she said, circling the spot and shoving the piece of paper toward me. I paid her and stepped back outside.

The rain seemed to be letting up, and I was anxious to make camp. By the time I'd backed into place, the rain had stopped completely, so I hauled the panels out of the trailer and set them up as quickly as I could. I knew Raven would be acting up if I didn't get him out of the trailer soon, and I didn't want to give the owner any reason to change her mind about letting us stay. I'd just gotten him settled with fresh water and a flake of hay from the back of the truck when the siren cut loose.

Almost immediately, Alice Boudreau burst out of the front door of the office, a huge red umbrella held over her head. As she began running from space to space, the clouds opened up again, huge drops of rain drenching everything in their path. The distant siren continued its wail as she dashed from camper to camper. When she finally reached me, she was soaking wet, out of breath, and her once meticulous hair hung in front of her face in damp clumps.

"There's a tornado coming," she yelled. "Get to the

shelter under the pavilion. It's the small building next to the office. Hurry! There isn't much time!" Then she turned around and practically ran back the way she had come.

"Wait, Mrs. Boudreau! Is there room for — I mean, can I bring..." She must not have heard me, or chose not to because she didn't turn around, nor did she slow down.

For a moment or two I just stood there, uncertain as to what to do. That is until the wind picked up, and hail started pelting me. I had no choice. I couldn't just leave Raven to the mercy of the weather, so I wrenched open the back of the trailer. After getting him situated in his stall, I secured the back door from the inside as best as I could. The sound of the hailstones on the metal roof was deafening; they had to be at least an inch in diameter. Raven shifted his weight from one foot to the other and moved back and forth. Not wanting to get stepped on or crushed by a panicking horse, I stayed on the other side of the divider and tried to calm him down.

The trailer creaked as the wind shoved against it, rolling it from side to side. I closed my eyes, trusting that the combined weight of the diesel truck and horse trailer was enough to keep the rig on the ground.

As the sound of the hail began to lessen, I became aware of a new sound. One that reminded me of the VRE as it approached the Brooke Station. I slid down the wall of the trailer; placing my forehead on my knees and wrapping my arms around my legs, I waited.

The trailer shuddered under the force of the gale, and Raven stamped his foot. Suddenly a swirling gust of wind whipped open one of the doors and slammed it against the side of the trailer. Air rushed in and around us, and I began to think I'd made a severe error in judgment. Not only about the storm, but also about the move — the change in career. Scott hadn't been exaggerating when he told me there wasn't much action in Modoc County. During my month of orientation there'd been no stakeouts, no high-speed chases. When a tractor was reported as stolen, we immediately drove to the location, anxious to solve the crime. But by the time we got there, it had been found parked in a different outbuilding on the ranch before we had a chance to investigate. I hated to admit it but maybe Sue had been right. Maybe I was making a terrible mistake.

Then I realized something else; the wind and hail had ceased, leaving only silence in their wake. I scrambled to my feet and stepped outside. The lack of sound and people made me feel like I was in one of Stephen King's apocalyptic novels. Hoping the danger had passed, I brought Raven out of the trailer again. Still agitated, he paced from one end of his tiny enclosure to the other. He reminded me of the young horse Scott and I'd been working with while I was living in Alturas. His Arabian blood made him high-spirited and hard to handle, but we enjoyed the challenge as well as the opportunity to get to know one another again. I hadn't realized how much I missed him.

"Easy boy," I said, grabbing hold of Raven's halter. I rubbed his huge, flat forehead. "You're all right. Just a little wind, that's all." *At least, I hope that's all.*

A few moments later, after I'd gotten him settled down, the others began to file out of the small octagonal building. Speaking in whispers, they meandered back to their temporary homes, collecting their scattered belongings as they went.

Still feeling a little shaken myself, I plugged in the trailer and climbed inside to turn on the fridge. Between the wind and Raven's panic attack, the side-to-side movement of the trailer had knocked some of the lighter things off the shelf, but no damage had been done. Back outside, I spotted Mrs. Boudreau, minus her umbrella, making her rounds at a little more leisurely pace. She'd attempted to return her hairdo to its original state but without much luck.

"Oh, I'm so glad you're okay," she said as she

approached. "I was worried when I noticed you hadn't followed me."

"I couldn't leave Raven. Are there any more storms heading this way?"

"The radio reported the worst of it is over. We may still get some rain, but that's all. I hope the rest of your stay is pleasant." Then she hustled away.

After what we've been through, it can only get better.

My stomach reminded me that I hadn't eaten since this morning, so I decided to splurge and have a frozen dinner and helping of bag o'salad. But first I had to replace the hay that had been blown out of the net and get Raven some clean water. Looking into the bed of my Dooley, I was glad I'd stretched a cargo net over it. The wind had tossed things about and blown the tarp loose, exposing the bale of hay, but nothing was missing.

As quickly as I could, I took care of Raven and tidied the bed of the truck. Then I climbed back into the trailer and started my own dinner. However, I'd had enough of small cramped places, so I sat in the cab of the truck to eat, using the console as a miniature table. Just as I was finishing, the rain began again. I hopped out and shimmied over the side of the makeshift corral. Then I grabbed Raven's blanket and managed to get it in place before the horse got too wet. Its oiled, canvas exterior and fleece lining would keep most of him dry and warm. I, on the other hand, was not as fortunate. Soaked clear through to my underwear, I retreated to the tiny sleeping quarters of the trailer and peeled off my wet clothes.

It was only the second day of my trip, but I felt like I'd been on the road for at least a week. And I wasn't looking forward to tomorrow. The next open KOA campground was in Cheyenne, Wyoming and that was at least eleven hours away. Tucked into my cozy little bed, I hoped for a restful night and an uneventful drive to my next stop.

Chapter 5

The rain, which has been falling for almost an hour is coming down harder now. Another crash of thunder brings the old man out of the cave. Looking across the creek bed, he sees his dog crawl out from under the car and hears its barking. "Damn dog never did like being out in the weather," he mutters to himself. "Chopper, shut up!" But the dog doesn't stop.

The old man adjusts the strap of his canvas knapsack and starts down the rock-strew hillside. He's almost to the bottom when his knee gives out, and he tumbles down the last ten feet. It takes him several minutes to get to his feet, and by now he's soaking wet. As he fords the creek, another rumble of thunder echoes down the canyon, but this one doesn't fade. Instead it grows louder.

Halfway across, the old man stops and looks upstream. A wall of water, well over his head, bears down on him. He turns, stumbles over a large rock, and falls. Hitting his head, he's knocked unconscious, and the water sweeps him away.

The wind howled and rain pounded the roof of the horse trailer all night. That, combined with the fear of another tornado touching down at any moment, had me so strung out the next morning, I felt like I'd been on a three-day stake out. I made the transition onto I-80 near Omaha and had settled into the flow of traffic when the trailer suddenly lurched like a gust of wind had hit it. Glancing in my side view mirror, I saw hunks of tire scattered all over the highway. I released a string of Sue's favorite curse words, pulled the rig over and began digging out the spare.

A passing truck driver helped me, and I located a tire shop in Lincoln. By the time I was back on the road, my eleven-hour day had grown to thirteen, and although it was after eight o'clock by the time I reached Cheyenne, I arrived there without any more mishaps.

A good night's sleep, an early start, and clear roads over the Rocky Mountains put me at the KOA campground in West Wendover, Nevada just before dark. If you could call it a campground. Situated between two casinos, it was like camping in a parking lot. Fortunately, it sat at the base of an enormous, mountain of rock, and I was able to secure a space toward the back in order to keep Raven away from traffic.

As my dinner heated in the microwave, I called Cindy Evans. With her green eyes, curly light brown hair, and smattering of freckles, she was a sharp contrast to Sue James but proved to be as good a friend. After knowing me for less than a week, she'd secured a place for me to stay during orientation. A room at her uncle's motel on the edge of Alturas, it came with a kitchenette and a discounted rate. She also volunteered to move my clothes, computer, and other odds and ends to my place in Fort Bidwell while I drove west.

"Modoc County Sheriff's Office." I recognized the dispatcher's voice right away.

"Cindy, it's Sarah."

"Hey, where are you?"

"West Wendover, Nevada. I should be in Fort Bidwell by tomorrow afternoon."

"How's your trip so far?"

"Uh... eventful. I'll fill you in the next time I see you. Let me just say I wish it was over."

"Sorry to hear that, but you'll be happy to know Scott

and I got your stuff all delivered, and the place looks great."

"Can't wait to see it. How are things at the office? Anything exciting happen while I've been gone?"

"Not a damn thing. Oh, I almost forgot; your unit is ready, and you can pick it up Monday. I'll have Scott come fetch you early that morning."

"Sounds good. Thanks for your help and I'll see you soon."

"You bet. Take care." Cindy disconnected.

My cell phone beeped at me. Low battery. I climbed into the cab of the truck and plugged it in. Feeling lonely, I called Sue.

"Sarah, I'm so glad you called," she said without even saying hello. "You'll never guess what happened at work?"

"I'm fine and how are you?"

"Quit kiddin' around. This is important."

"Okay, what's got you so excited?"

"Hensley got..." A blast from the horn of a passing truck drowned out her voice.

"What about Hensley?"

"The deputy director fired his ass."

"He did? Why?"

"What do you mean why? Your report, that's why. Apparently he's been under review since you turned it in."

"Really?"

"Yeah, and they interviewed a whole bunch of people. You should have heard Hensley rant and rave. He called the deputy director every name in the book and threatened to beat him up. Finally, they escorted him out of the building."

"What about his henchman?"

"Morgan? I heard they gave him Hensley's job. So how's the trip with Raven going?"

"Horrible." I quickly relayed the details of my journey.

"Well..." she said when I was finished, "you could always come back, what with Hensley gone and all."

For a brief second I actually considered it, but the thought of enduring another trip cross-country brought me back to my senses. "I'd be willing to bet the Bureau hasn't seen the last of Hensley. Besides, I can't disappoint Sheriff Atkins."

"What did you say his name was?"

"Chet Atkins."

Sue giggled. "Not *the* Chet Atkins?"

"What's so funny?"

"Chet Atkins is a famous country western singer. My dad used to listen to him all the time, but he must be about a hundred by now."

Suddenly I understood why Scott always got a funny look on his face, like he was expecting me to say something, every time someone spoke the Sheriff's name. "Different Chet Atkins," I said flatly.

"No kiddin'!" She roared with laughter. "So where are you and when will you get to Surprise Valley?" she asked when she'd finally composed herself.

"Nevada and tomorrow. If I get out of here by seven in the morning, I'll have plenty of time to get Raven settled and unpack a few things from my place in Alturas before the movers arrive."

"Well, good luck and call me when you get there."

"Thanks, I will. Bye." I left my phone to charge and went to check on my dinner. The enchiladas were still frozen in the middle and the refried beans looked like something I'd scrape off my shoe. I needed some real Mexican food. And a beer. After making sure Raven was set for the night, I headed for the casinos in search of a cerveza and the biggest chimichanga I could find.

A gunshot! Where did it come from? Stepping out of the black SUV, I look around. A flash of light to the left draws my attention. I can see the shooter now, standing in the shadows of the old building. He raises his gun, a large rifle of some kind. Another gunshot shatters the silence. I see the bullet coming; it's in slow motion. Sliding to one side, I move out of its way. The shooter steps closer; I can almost see his face. He's taking aim and another shot rings out. Again the bullet comes in slow motion, but my attention is on the man. Who is he? The lights of a passing car catch him. Hensley! But why is he shooting at me?

Another loud bang and I was wide-awake. The sound reverberated through the trailer and made my head throb. Coming to a sitting position, the pounding in my head increased. Memories of last night slowly crept into my brain. Too many cervezas. Last thing I could remember was singing with some big guy dressed like a cowboy. *Thank goodness I'm just passing through!*

More banging and I realized it was Raven smacking the side of the trailer with his hoof. The horse had no patience at all. Looking at my watch, I knew why. It was past eight-thirty and I was going to be late. I jumped out of bed and wasn't surprised to see I was still wearing yesterday's clothes. I put my shoes back on and headed for the bathroom. I did what I needed to, splashed cold water on my face, and returned to the truck. We had to get on the road as soon as possible.

Although Raven wanted to get out of his small pen, he balked when I tried to load him into the trailer. "Come on boy," I coaxed, "we're almost home. Just a few more hours and you'll have a green pasture to run around in." When he stood at the back of the trailer looking at me, I knew I had to try a different approach. I quickly tied him to the door and climbed back into my tiny living quarters. I grabbed the bag of carrots from the fridge and tore it open, scattering them everywhere. Armed with three of the long, orange vegetables, I prepared to do battle with the stubborn gelding.

Lead rope in hand, I showed him the treat and tried to guide him inside. Instead of following me, he lowered his massive head and took a step backward. No matter how many commands I used, he wouldn't budge. I climbed back out and led him in a big circle and tried again to load him. After the fourth time and no luck, I shook the carrots at him and threw them into the trailer. Without hesitating, he stepped up and moved right into position, eating carrots as he went. Now I had to kick it into high gear.

I locked the divider into place and loaded the panels with break-neck speed. Next I cleaned up what Raven had left behind during the night, unplugged the trailer, and climbed into the cab of my Ford Dooley. Fort Bidwell was over seven hours away. The moving van was scheduled to arrive at four o'clock that afternoon, and it was almost nine-thirty when I pulled out of the KOA.

We made good time on Interstate 80, driving right at the posted speed limit. As I approached the exit for Highway 95 just outside Winnemucca, a large Bekins moving van with Virginia license plates passed me, making no effort to move to the right, and went past the exit. The race was on, and my only hope was that their route would take longer than mine.

Turning left at the junction of state route 140, I made it as far as Denio, Nevada before my stomach insisted I get something to eat. Not wanting anything that resembled Mexican food, I settled for a tuna sandwich and a diet soda from the deli counter of a small grocery store, which I ate on the road. By three-thirty, I was in California and starting up Cedar Pass, but Fort Bidwell was at least an hour away.

Pulling through Cedarville, a horse trailer in tow, gave me a feeling of home. Scott and I had done the same thing at least a dozen times during our rodeo days, but instead of turning right and heading for the fairgrounds, I turned north and started for my new place.

Liz Leerman, the realtor Sheriff Atkins recommended, had called me one afternoon, all excited that she'd found me the perfect house. I was skeptical when I learned it was in Fort Bidwell rather than the more centrally located

Cedarville, but I was willing to check it out. The property was set back away from any main roads and included five acres, most of which was pasture. The house itself was a small run-down building with two bedrooms, one bath, living room and kitchen. The laundry room consisted of a washer and dryer squeezed into a small pump house about thirty feet from the back door, and there was a small barn with a stall for Raven. What convinced me to buy was the bathhouse, which was a small building built halfway between the barn and the house. It covered a pit lined with round, river rocks set in cement and was filled by a hot spring. It was the best feature the property had to offer and a luxury I'd been looking forward to since buying the place.

As I traveled along the shallow alkaline lakes of Surprise Valley, I searched for the moving van. The flatness of the valley floor allowed for clear visibility in all directions, but the large white and green semi-truck was nowhere in sight. I kept my fingers crossed as I continued driving north.

When I turned off the county road, I began to get excited. Cindy's cousin, one of her many relatives living in Modoc County, had been hired to paint the entire house, and the flooring place in Alturas was supposed to install the new carpeting. I hoped Cindy's report of how good it looked wasn't an exaggeration.

Pulling down the driveway, my first reaction was that I had the wrong place. The house looked better than I had imagined; its new coat of pale green paint made it look quaint and inviting. Better than that, the moving van hadn't beaten me, so I had time to unload Raven and check out the house.

It took three tries, but I finally got the horse trailer backed in next to the barn. I unlatched the gate, opened the door of the trailer, and patted the large gelding on the rump. Snorting and tossing his head, he backed out. I grabbed his lead rope and guided him through the gate.

"Well, Raven," I said, rubbing his huge flat forehead.

"This is our new home." I unbuckled his halter and pulled it off. The horse spun away from me and trotted across the field, his thick main ruffled by the breeze. Watching him prance back and forth along the far fence line, I knew it would be several days before he'd even get close enough for me to pet him, let alone put his halter back on.

Leaving the diesel Ford Dooley where it was, I walked the short distance to the house and unlocked the front door. The smell of fresh paint and new carpet washed over me like a tsunami. I opened all the windows and doors, hoping the smell would dissipate by the time I was ready to go to sleep. Breathing a little easier, I wandered through the house again and was pleasantly surprised at how well it had turned out. Replacing the odd collection of worn carpets, a different one in each room, with a layer of cinnamon-colored plush carpeting made the house look larger, one room flowing into the next. The only flooring I didn't have replaced was the miniature brick pattern in the kitchen and sunroom. Similar to what had been in my mother's kitchen, it reminded me of home.

As I moved through the house, I mentally arranged the furniture until I had a pretty good idea where things would go. Then I went back outside. Still no moving van. *Don't tell me they got lost.* Checking my watch, I walked back to the Ford in search of my cell phone. I had just punched in the number when the Bekins truck crept around the corner. I snapped the phone shut and walked down the driveway to meet them, hoping the driver was better at backing up than I was.

As soon as the moving van was in position, the two men climbed down out of the cab. "Man, talk about being in the middle of nowhere," the driver said, as he walked over to where I was waiting. According to the patch on his shirt, his name was Don.

"Yes, it's a little isolated," I replied.

"Isolated?" He shoved his ball cap to the back of his head. "Lady this place isn't even on the map!"

"Good one!" his partner said, clapping him on the back.

"You liked that, eh Shorty?"

Before things went from bad to worse, I interrupted. "The doors are open if you'd like to get started."

"Yeah, sure lady. Whatever you say." The men moved to the side of the enormous trailer, slid open the door, and began getting the ramp into place.

Peering into the dark interior, I silently greeted my belongings like old friends. I couldn't wait to sit on my own couch and watch my own television, but the thing I'd missed most was my bed. The firm queen-size mattress, which sat on a frame made of dark wood, had always provided a good night's sleep. The same couldn't be said of the small, lumpy mattress I'd been sleeping on at the motel in Alturas.

One by one, my things were unloaded and carted into the house. "Where do you want this?" Don asked, as the two men struggled with my Tae Kwon Do sparring dummy. Not only was it heavy, the paddles that stuck out to resemble human appendages made it difficult to carry. "Your husband work out?"

"No husband. It's mine."

"Yeah right." Shorty gave his partner the all-knowing wink.

I considered giving him a quick demonstration but decided it wasn't worth the effort. "Put it in the back bedroom." While they finished emptying out the van, I unhitched the horse trailer and began cleaning it out.

After stripping the linen from the small cot, I rolled the rest of the laundry inside the sheets and carried it up to the house. It took a few minutes to hook up the washer and dryer, but I managed and started a load. The mini-fridge was next. I threw away the last Mexican TV dinner and bag of wilted lettuce but kept the three half-thawed burritos along with the bottled water and flavored green tea, which I hauled to the kitchen and shoved into the fridge. By the time I had it plugged in and pushed into place, the movers were finished.

"We're all done, lady." Don held out a clipboard. "Just need you to look inside the van to see that nothing got left behind and check your things for any possible damage. If there's no problems then sign here." He pointed to the bottom of the page.

By six o'clock, I'd made my inspection, signed the necessary forms, and Tweedle Dee and Tweedle Dum were pulling out of the driveway. I unpacked most of the boxes Cindy had brought over from Alturas but left the rest for morning. Except for the bed. After getting it put together, I dug through two boxes before I found the sheets and blankets I wanted.

Fighting the urge to lie down, I poked through the cupboards for something to eat. Flavored instant rice, a package of baking soda, and a box of herbal tea, with a single teabag, were the only edible things I found. A trip to the grocery store would be my next priority.

I filled a small pan with water — the teakettle was still packed — and pulled out the last teabag. Leaving the water to heat, I ran down to the bathhouse and checked out the tub. With the anticipation of a young child, I rinsed it out, put the carved wooden plug into place, and turned on the faucet. Back at the house I made a cup of tea, sat on the porch and waited for the tub to fill.

Completely enclosed with large windows, the front porch was more of a sunroom and would make a good office. As I mentally planned out the next two days, a vehicle pulled down the driveway. *Now what?* I opened the front door and waited for the early model Toyota Land Cruiser to come to a stop. A man definitely past middle age got out and waved. His green plaid shirt was tucked into faded blue jeans, which just touched the tops of a pair of brown work boots. He reached back into the rig and retrieved a pie plate. "Howdy," he said, brushing his felt hat with the fingertips of his free hand. "Name's Remy Hamilton."

"Sarah Murdock," I called through the screen door. "What can I do for you?"

"I live over yonder in that mobile on the hill," he said, pointing in the direction of the main road. "Saw you moving in and thought you might like a house warming gift." He held up the dish and nodded toward the side of the house. "Apple pie made from the best apples around."

I opened the screen door and came down the steps. "From my trees?" I asked, looking at my miniature orchard.

"Yep. 'Course I picked them some time ago. Hated to see them going to waste. Is your man around? Bet he'd enjoy a piece. My own secret recipe."

What is it with men assuming I'm half of a couple? I forced a smile. "No man here."

"You live alone?"

I nodded.

"Hmm." About my height, his face was hidden behind a short white beard and trimmed mustache, but he looked harmless enough.

"Would you like to come in?" I asked.

"Don't mind if I do." He walked past me and up the steps. The smell of apples and cinnamon enveloped me, and I followed him and the pie into the kitchen. After placing the dessert on the table, he settled himself in one of the chairs. "So what brings you to Surprise Valley?"

Nothing like getting right to the point. "I'm starting a new job here in a few days," I said, sitting across from him.

"Really? What do you do?"

I thought about what to tell him. "You could say I'm in public relations. Can I offer you a cup of coffee?" I'd unpacked the coffeemaker but wasn't sure there was any coffee tucked away in one of the remaining boxes stacked along the kitchen wall.

"Only if it's decaf. Had to give up the leaded kind. Maybe you have something stronger?"

I shook my head. "Sorry." An ice-cold beer sounded good to me, too. "I'd offer you some tea, but I'm afraid I used my last teabag. How about some pie?" I said, getting to my feet. Fortunately there were paper plates and plastic utensils left over from living in the motel.

I cut each of us a generous piece of the still warm pie. "This smells delicious."

Remy watched as I took my first bite. Instantly I was whisked back in time to my grandmother's kitchen. Summers spent romping through her apple orchards; helping her make apple pies for Thanksgiving dinner. "Well?" he asked.

I rolled my eyes. "This tastes like..." I searched for the perfect word to describe the spicy sweet bite as I savored it in my mouth. Only one thing came to mind. "...home!"

He beamed. "Glad you like it. It's taken me almost two years to get the crust just right. Still isn't as good as the missus used to make."

"She doesn't bake anymore?"

Remy removed his hat and placed it over his heart. "Peg's been gone for over ten years now."

"Oh, I'm so sorry," I stammered. *Leave it to me to say the wrong thing.*

"No harm done," he said, replacing the hat on his head. Then he had a bite of his own pie. "Yep, that's how it's supposed to taste."

After we finished, Remy stood. "Well, I should be going," he said and moved out onto the porch.

"Thanks for coming by and thanks for the pie." I followed him to the front door and watched as he drove up the driveway. Then I remembered the tub. I hurried back into the kitchen, cut myself another piece, grabbed what was left of my cold tea, and headed for the bathhouse.

Stepping inside the tiny building, I set my cup and plate on the edge of the rustic tub, peeled off my clothes and slipped into the water. I have always enjoyed a good soak but feeling the warm water flow over my body was sheer heaven. Any doubts I had about moving back to California and starting a new career melted away. I was home. *Thank you, Hensley. You actually did me a favor.*

Chapter 6

"I tell you I haven't seen him for a week. What with all the sandbagging and pulling crap out of the culverts, I haven't had time to take a piss, let alone check on an old man."

The tall man swirls his shot of whiskey before swallowing it in one gulp. "Don't worry about it. He's probably visiting his sister. He'll turn up sooner or later."

"Well he better hurry his ass up. I still got three boxes to sort and his place is locked up tight."

The next morning I awoke to the sound of twittering songbirds. It took me a few moments to realize where I was, but when I did I stretched my arms over my head. Sleep hadn't felt that good for weeks, and if I didn't have the huge job of unpacking looming over me, I'd have stayed in bed. Unfortunately I didn't have that option.

A cup of hot coffee was essential, so I started with the last of the boxes from Alturas. A small red can lay in the bottom of one of them with barely enough coffee for half of a pot. With the eagerness of a sterno drunk, I caressed my cup and took a sip. The brown liquid wasn't as strong as I liked, but it tasted good all the same.

As I finished my first cup, I wandered through the house, making a mental list of what had to be done. The stereo and television had to be hooked up, and my CDs needed to be unpacked and put into the rack. All my books had to be arranged on the bookshelf and the computer set up. That alone would take most of the morning. The boxes of clothes, bathroom supplies, and kitchen items should finish off the day. After a second cup of coffee and another piece of pie, I was ready to begin.

Several hours later the house was put together, more or less, and a mountain of empty boxes had grown outside the back door. I was tired and hungry and needed something to eat besides pie, so I grabbed my keys and headed south on County Road 1.

Entering Cedarville, I spotted Morrison's Mercantile on the right and guided the big truck to the side of the road. Before getting out, I checked my image in the rearview mirror. A day of unpacking boxes and re-arranging furniture had loosened my hair from its bondage. Not wanting to take the time to re-braid it, I pulled the band off and ran my fingers through the long brown hair. *Not glamorous but a definite improvement.* I stepped down from the vehicle, stretched my legs and went inside.

Walking around the small grocery store, I felt like I'd been transported back in time. The well-worn, oiled floorboards of the rustic store creaked as I moved across them. A small meat counter ran across the back of the long, narrow building and the freestanding shelves were short enough to look over.

A connoisseur of frozen entrées and Mexican take-out, I was afraid they wouldn't have much to choose from. Fortunately they had bag o'salad, so I picked up one along with a bottle of bleu cheese dressing. It was a good start, and I kept browsing. As I passed the freestanding cooler, I grabbed a twelve pack of Michelob. Then I selected a few cans of chili, a small brick of cheddar cheese, a jar of peanut butter, and a loaf of bread. For breakfast I settled on PopTarts, cereal bars, a gallon of milk, and two containers of coffee — one regular and one instant, in case I didn't have time to wait for the coffee maker.

Hefting the bags of groceries into the back of the truck, I glanced up the road. A neon mug, complete with a head of foam, flashed at me from the single window of the Silver Spur Saloon. The trucks parked in front, many of which were at least twenty years old and sporting dents of various sizes and shapes, suggested it was a favorite place of the local ranchers. Not only would it be a perfect opportunity to meet some of the residents, an ice-cold beer sounded real good.

I made my way across the street and went inside, my eyes slowly adjusting to the dim light. The walls were covered with a patchwork of paneling, probably replacing the oddments of the occasional bar fight. Way in the back, an old pool table sat within the dim circle of light radiating from a dusty Coors lamp. Behind the bar an enormous elk head and metal signs advertising Chesterfield and Pall Mall cigarettes put the finishing touches on the place. As I strolled over to the nearest bar stool and sat down, I could feel eyes staring at me from all directions. *Should have left my hair pulled back.*

"What'll ya have?" the bartender asked. A two-tone bowling shirt hung loosely on his six-foot frame. Not a day over thirty, his mustache and Elvis style sideburns were as black as his hair and connected by five o'clock shadow. His crystal-blue eyes sparkled.

Bottles of Budweiser were scattered across the top of the bar. "I'll have a Bud," I said, hoping to blend in. He popped the top on a tall brown bottle and set it down in front of me. I took a long draw. *Oh yeah, that hits the spot.* Perhaps fitting into this cozy community wasn't going to be so hard after all.

"Come here often?" a voice asked from behind.

I closed my eyes. "No, this is my first visit." Hoping to terminate the conversation, I stared straight ahead and took another sip of beer.

A lanky man with long stringy hair sat down on the stool next to me, the faint smell of bovine excrement following close behind. Looking down, I saw that his worn-out cowboy boots had an ample sprinkling of it. *Perfect accessory for the outfit.* Unlike the ranchers who were wearing Wranglers and short sleeve shirts, this guy had on Levis that should have had a decent burial years ago and a T-shirt so tattered it would have made a marginal rag. I shuddered to think when he'd bathed last.

"Come on, Bill," the bartender said, drifting back down the bar. "Leave the lady alone."

"Just being friendly," Bill said. "Nothing wrong with being friendly. Right?"

I knew he was looking at me, waiting for an answer, but I continued to stare at my reflection in the grimy mirror hanging behind the bar.

"So, what's your sign?"

"Look," I said, turning to Bill. "I'm sure you're a..." I searched for the right word. "Nice guy." I paused. "But I just want to sit here and drink my beer. So if you don't mind..."

"Oh, well excuse me your highness," Bill said, getting to his feet. Without realizing it, he'd stepped down inside the legs of my stool.

"Wait!"

"Oh no," Bill said, waving me off. "You had your chance lady, no second..." Down he went in a tangled heap, and laughter erupted throughout the room.

"Shut up!" he said, scrambling to his feet. "Shut the hell up! You're all a bunch of assholes."

"Come on, Bill," the bartender said, grinning from ear to ear. "It was just an accident and, you got to admit, it was damn funny."

"Funny? How about I trash this place?" He picked up a barstool and held it over his head. "Now that'd be funny!"

"If you don't calm down, I'm going to have to ask you to leave."

"I ain't going nowhere." He shook the stool at the bartender. "I pay for my beers same as everybody else, and you ain't throwing me outta here!"

The bartender nodded toward the back of the room.

Turning around, I could just make out the silhouette of a very large man getting to his feet.

"What'll it be, Bill? You gonna calm yourself down or does Hank need to escort your ass out of here?"

"This ain't over!" Bill sent the stool crashing against the bar, leaving a deep gash in the wood. "You'll see! Someday I might just buy this place and kick all you assholes outta here." He turned and stormed out the door.

"Sorry about that," the bartender said as he came around the end of the bar. He righted the stool and sat down next to me.

"Thanks for your help."

"My pleasure, I'm sure. So, are you new to the area or just passing through?"

"I bought a house north of here."

"Really? What do you do?"

I paused, my beer halfway to my lips.

"Oh, sorry. Just making conversation. Didn't mean to get too personal." He swung off the stool and went about collecting empties.

I took another long draw on my beer.

"What's a nice girl like you doing in a place like this?"

Unbelievable. Don't these guys have any better pick up lines? Slowly I lowered the bottle. "Look, I just want to sit here and..."

A deep chuckle erupted from a man in a blue plaid shirt. "Relax, he said as he sat next to me. "I don't bite."

"Mr. Hamilton!"

"Oh please, call me Remy." He removed his black felt hat and laid it on the stool next to him.

"All right — Remy. I'm sorry. I thought you were another..."

"Another what?"

"Never mind," I said, shaking my head. I drained my beer and set the empty bottle on the bar.

"I thought you didn't drink anything stronger than tea?"

"Only when there's nothing else in the house."

"Glad to hear it," he said, finishing off his own drink. "Pete," he called down the bar, "how about another one?" The bartender filled Remy's glass with an amber-colored liquor. "This here's my new neighbor, Sarah," he said, nodding toward me.

"Pleased to meet you," Pete said, flashing me a big smile. "Ready for another one?" He picked up my empty bottle.

"No thanks. I've got to get going." I slid off the barstool and started for the door. "See you later, Remy."

Responding to a call in the pre-dawn hours has always made me nervous. Maybe it was because any sane person was home in bed. Maybe it was because the most heinous crimes seem to take place then. Maybe it was just a residual effect from watching horror movies as a teenager on the late, late show. Whatever the reason, tonight was no exception.

The phone rang just before three o'clock and, although I was technically off-duty and without a patrol unit, a situation had come up that no one else was available to handle. Not really knowing what to expect, I'd left the comfort of my warm bed, pulled on my uniform, and set out on my quest.

It didn't take me long to find the place, and when I pulled down the narrow driveway, the headlights shone on the guy I was probably looking for. He stood in front of a small trailer, arm cocked back, ready to launch the rock he had in his hand. Startled by the lights, he threw it at me instead, and it bounced off the windshield of my Ford Dooley.

Shit! I slammed on the brakes and shut down the engine. I slid out of the cab and stepped to the front of the truck. "Get on the ground and spread your arms and legs!" I yelled.

"Go to hell!" The man bent over and selected another rock.

I released the snap on my holster. "I said hit the ground! Now!"

He stepped toward me, squinting in the bright light. "Just who the hell are... YOU! What are you doing here? And in that uniform? You got to be shittin' me."

The long stringy hair and tattered clothing were unmistakable. I pulled my Sig 9mm from its holster and pointed it in his direction. "Bill, we can do this the easy way or we can do this the hard way. Hit the dirt now!"

A sinister grin crossed his face, as he lay spread-eagle on the ground. "Whatever you say — Deputy!"

With him secure in the backseat of my Ford, I began the long journey over Cedar Pass to the county jail. Even with all the windows open, the smell was unbearable. Not exactly the best start to a new career.

Chapter 7

Deputy Scott Jenkins rapped on my door prior to sun-up Monday morning. Since sleep had abandoned me long before that, I was dressed and ready to go. After a quick trip over Cedar Pass and back, I had my unit and was ready to start my patrol. Well, almost — the PopTart I'd devoured on the way hadn't lasted very long, and I needed something to eat.

Parking the county-issued Ford Explorer in front of the Wagon Wheel Café, I looked across Middle Lake. Crusty patches of alkali trimmed the outer edges of the shallow lake, and the sun was just barely visible over the high plateau. The eastern slope of the Warner Mountains formed a natural barrier on the other side of the narrow valley. A rugged range decorated with gigantic pines and jagged outcroppings of volcanic rock, it was the kind of country Raven and I would enjoy exploring.

I adjusted my gun belt and pushed through the door, the bell tinkling against the glass. The few customers seated inside looked up long enough to see if nods of recognition were required. But after realizing the new arrival was a stranger, they returned to their meals.

A low counter covered with pink and green Formica ran down one side, and small booths with upholstery sporting the same pastel color scheme lined the other. The charcoal gray floor glistened beneath numerous coats of Johnson's wax. The place reminded me of a diner my family and I visited every Friday night in Red Bluff.

My newly acquainted neighbor, Remy Hamilton, wearing a red plaid shirt, was seated at the counter, his black hat perched on one knee. I sauntered over and sat down next to him. He glanced my way and then did a double take. "Well, I'll be damned. Public relations, huh?"

"Yeah, sort of," I said, pushing my sunglasses up like a headband.

"So, how long have you been a deputy?"

"I've been in law enforcement for several years but just started as a deputy."

"What'd you do before?"

I had to hand it to Remy; he sure wasn't one to beat around the bush. "I worked in Washington D.C. With the FBI."

"Well, what the hell are you doing in Surprise Valley?"

"Ordering breakfast," I said, pulling a menu out the rack. Chicken fried steak, biscuits and gravy, three-egg omelets made with fresh ranch eggs. If I weren't careful, I'd weigh three hundred pounds inside of six months. "Excuse me, do you have any fresh fruit or bagels?" I called to the waitress at the other end of the counter. Her hesitation told me the café didn't serve such things and probably wouldn't be doing so in the near future. "Never mind. Could you just bring me some dry wheat toast and coffee, please?"

Remy sat very still, cradling his cup in both hands and staring straight ahead.

"What?" I asked after a few moments of silence.

"Just thinking," he said, lowering his cup to the counter. "You used to work in a big city for the FBI and now you're in a ranching community in the sticks, playing deputy sheriff." Turning to look at me, he continued. "And you don't want to talk about it. Strikes me as mighty peculiar."

Oh great, my new neighbor is an armchair Columbo. "At least not right now." The waitress brought my coffee and a small chrome pitcher of cream so cold moisture had collected on the outside. A packet of sugar and a shot of the cream made the hearty, diner-style cup of coffee just right. "Some other time," I promised, "over a couple of cold ones."

"Fair enough," he said, going back to his bacon and eggs. "So then, I'll bet you were the one that went out on that call the other night."

"Now how did you...?" The arrival of my toast interrupted me, so I paused long enough to slather each slice with strawberry jam.

"Got me one of them scanners. All they said was to land line the new deputy about some guy chucking rocks."

"Yeah, it was my buddy, Bill, from the bar. I hauled him over to Alturas to sleep it off."

Remy laughed. "That would've been fun to watch. Was he glad to see you?"

"Not exactly."

"Who was he chucking rocks at?"

"I'm not sure. The person who called didn't want to press charges, just wanted him off the property."

"Where was it?"

"At a trailer off Laxaque Road."

"Old fence, narrow driveway?"

"That's the place."

Remy finished off his last bite, wiped his mouth and tossed the crumbled napkin onto his plate. "Belongs to Pete, the bartender over at the Silver Spur. Probably figured it'd be cheaper in the long run. That Bill's got some temper. No telling what he might do if pushed too far."

"I'll keep that in mind if I come across him again." I finished my toast and ordered a second coffee to go. "I'll see you, Remy," I said tucking a couple of dollars under the edge of my plate. Then I met the waitress at the cash register, added cream and sugar to my coffee-to-go, and paid my tab.

"I'll talk to you later," Remy called. "Good luck."

"Thanks," I said, stepping out the door and into the bright sunlight.

As I patrolled the area south of Cedarville, the first thing I noticed was how uncommonly friendly everyone was, waving as I drove by. Having been on the east coast for the last eight years, I had become accustomed to ignoring others and being ignored. The second thing I noticed was the stark beauty of the valley. I really hadn't paid that much attention to it when I'd come to Cedarville in high school — what high school student would. But now, the robin-egg blue of the sky, the enormity of the mountains, the vastness of the three alkali lakes stacked one upon the other... Perhaps living a quiet existence in this small community was what I needed.

After turning around at the county line, I'd just passed through Eagleville and was hoping to grab a bite to eat when I got a call over the radio.

"Unit 113, Modoc County."

"Go ahead Modoc, this is 113."

"We've got an 11-44 at the edge of Upper Lake where Goose Creek empties into it. RP is on scene. Look for a red Dodge Ram."

"Copy that. I'm just passing the airport. ETA is about 15 minutes."

"Copy, 113. Time is 12:28.

A dead body. I could feel the adrenaline as it entered my bloodstream. So much for the quiet, sleepy community where nothing exciting happens.

I turned onto a small dirt road that snaked across the barren field toward a stand of willow trees. The red pickup was parked off to the right along with three other vehicles, and a group of about ten people huddled close by. Apparently Remy wasn't the only one with a scanner.

As I got out of the Ford Explorer, a mountain of a man, his silhouette vaguely familiar, stepped away from the group and walked toward me. "So you're the new deputy?" he asked when he got close enough. "Believe I saw you at the Silver Spur the other day."

"That's right." I gave his hand a firm shake. "Deputy Murdock."

"Name's Hank Henrickson. My boy's the one that found it," he said nodding toward the crowd. "He was out riding the four-wheeler. I expect the person's been dead for a spell."

"Let's have a look." As I approached, the crowd's excited chatter dropped off to a quiet whisper.

"Afternoon folks. I'm Deputy Murdock." They exchanged glances. "Who found the body?"

A boy around the age of fifteen crept forward, his freckles accentuated by his pale face. "I did," he said, brushing his red hair out of his blue-green eyes.

I moved over closer to him and gave him my best smile. "Think you could show me where?" I asked, resting my hand on his shoulder. I remembered how freaked out I was the first time I saw a dead body outside of a funeral home.

He nodded, and we proceeded toward the willows growing along the creek. Stopping at the edge, he pointed toward a clump of bushes growing out of a high spot in the middle. I could just make out the leg of a pair of jeans and a black boot partially hidden among the vegetation.

I slid down the bank and waded across the shallow stream. A large sagebrush and several willow saplings had managed to establish themselves on the miniature island. The body lay at the base of them on the upstream side; dead leaves and twigs were packed around it.

"You didn't you touch anything, did you?" I called to the boy. Still watching from the edge of the creek, he shook his head. "Good." I crawled back up the bank and retrieved my gear from the patrol unit. Returning to the crowd, I placed the silver case on the ground and pulled out my notebook.

"Any idea who this might be?" Heads shook. "Okay, what's the flow of water like in this creek?" It didn't seem like the body had been dumped there, so maybe it had washed downstream from somewhere else.

"Usually it ain't much, but this past winter there was a heck of a flood around Lake City. This here creek in particular created quite a mess for us ranchers that live in the area." Nods and whispers confirmed Hank's story. "It was probably a month or two before the rains passed and the water level dropped back down to normal."

"I see." I put my notebook away. "I'm going to take a few pictures and then examine the area for evidence. When I'm done, I could use some help getting the body secured, if one or two of you could stick around." Another low murmur rolled through the crowd.

"I reckon I can give you a hand," Hank offered.

"I'd appreciate that. The rest of you folks can go on home."

More muttering, but no one moved.

"Suit yourselves," I told them, picking up my case. "But when I start moving that body around, there will definitely be a foul odor and pieces may fall off." *That ought to get them moving.* Looks of horror, more murmuring, and the crowd began to wander back to their cars parked nearby. Even Hank and his son looked uneasy.

"Give me about ten minutes." I slipped back down the bank and, after removing my camera from the case, made several trips around the body, snapping pictures. That done I pulled on a pair of latex gloves and began clearing the leaves away. A torn flannel shirt and tuft of white hair convinced me I was looking at the body of an old man. Not finding anything unusual, I uncovered the body as best I could.

"Okay, I'm ready," I called as I pulled out a black body bag and got it into position.

Hank started down the bank, his son close behind him. "Billy, you stay here. No need for you to watch this."

"Ah, Dad."

"Mind me, boy," Hank said as he continued across the creek.

"We're just going to kind of roll him onto this."
I handed the big man a pair of gloves. "Try breathing through your mouth; that should make it easier." *But not much I'm afraid.*

"Can pieces really fall off?" Hank asked, his face as pale as his son's.

"Of course not," I lied. "Grab hold of his clothes and we'll gently roll him over on the count of three. Ready? One, two, three..."

There was an odd popping sound and the lower half moved, but the shoulders wouldn't budge. Pulling more twigs and leaves away from the body, I could see some kind of strap holding him in place. I reached in behind him, took hold, and gave it a good tug. A loud snap and the corpse flopped over onto the body bag, face up, or at least the top part of him was face up. An old canvas knapsack lay on the ground next to him.

"Oh gross!" Hank and I turned to find Billy standing behind us, both hands covering his nose. "He sure does stink. Why is he all shiny? Looks like one of those guys in a wax museum."

"I'm guessing he's been underwater a long time," I said, grateful my stomach was empty.

"I told you to wait up top," Hank said to his son.

"But Dad, doesn't he kinda look like Gus?" Billy tilted his head to one side to get a better look. "In a grotesque sort of way. I mean his face is all bloated like, but doesn't he?"

Hank took another look. "Well, now that you mention it son, he does."

"Who's Gus?" I asked, stepping back for some fresh air and getting out my notebook again.

"An old guy that nobody's seen for a few months. Guess now we know why."

"Does Gus have a last name?"

"Miller."

I tucked the notebook back in my pocket, picked up the canvas bag, and looked inside. "You don't by any chance happen to know where these might have come from?" I asked, pulling out some kind a woven mat and unrolling it. Inside were three pieces of bone with notches cut into them, a large chunk of chiseled obsidian, and a section of deer antler.

"I know what those are," Billy said. "Some guys from the reservation came to our class last spring. These here are Indian artifacts. You know, the kinds of things they bury with their dead."

"Was Gus Native American?"

"Ah, hell no. He hated those guys," Billy said.

Hank scowled at his son. "Mind that mouth of yours, boy."

"Sorry, Dad. Wonder how come Gus would have them?" Billy asked, seeming eager to change the subject.

"An excellent question," I said, re-rolling the items in the mat and sliding it back into the bag. "Let's get old Gus here zipped up and loaded into my vehicle."

A few minutes later, I was making another trip to Alturas. I needed to find out who or what had killed this guy, and I was willing to bet it had something to do with the contents of the canvas knapsack.

Chapter 8

It was almost two o'clock by the time I arrived at the Sheriff's Office, and I still hadn't eaten lunch. I found someone to help me unload Gus and left the knapsack and roll of film with Josh Green, our only lab tech. Then I went to check-in with Cindy.

"Hey, Sarah," she said as I rounded the corner and stopped at her desk. "How was it?"

"Pretty routine recovery — not too bad. I was hoping to speak with the sheriff. Is he around?"

"He had a meeting at City Hall earlier. Hold on a second." She rolled her chair to the right and picked up the duty roster. "He's due back in a few minutes, if you want to hang around."

"Yeah, sure. I'll grab a soda or something." I wandered into the break room and perused the vending machines.

"What are you doing back on this side of the mountain so soon?" It was Scott.

"A dead body," I said, dropping some change into the slot and punching in the combination to a bag of Corn Nuts and a Snickers bar.

"Oh, quick jerking my chain. Why are you really here?"

"I'm serious. I recovered the remains of an old man." I fished my snack out of the bottom compartment of the vending machine and turned around. "I'm waiting for the sheriff to return so I can brief him."

His eyes squinted and his crooked smile appeared.

"Must be giving a concert somewhere. No wait. I've got it. He's out tuning up his guitar." He chuckled.

I rolled my eyes. "Not funny, Scott."

"Oh, so now you get it?" He looked around and leaned closer. "You know how he got that name, don't you?"

I shook my head as I bit into my candy bar.

"Apparently his mother was a real fan of country and western music, and when she married a guy named Atkins, she couldn't resist naming her son Chet." He began to chuckle. "Know what's even funnier? I hear the sheriff hasn't got a musical bone in his body." His chuckling turned into laughter.

"Uh, Scott..." Something behind him had caught my attention. I furrowed my brow and gave him the slightest shake of my head, but Scott was not one to catch on quickly. When his laugh finally began to subside, Sheriff Atkins cleared his throat.

"Oh God!" Scott face blanched. Then he closed his eyes, took a deep breath, and turned around. "Sheriff..."

"Save it Jenkins." Shifting his eyes to meet mine, the sheriff continued. "I understand we have a body to transport to Redding."

"Yes sir. I think...

"Just a moment," he said, holding up one hand. "Let me get Jenkins on his way."

"On my way sir? But I just came off shift. I..."

"Load the body into the van and drive it to Redding. Now."

"Yes, sir." Scott wasn't smiling anymore. "See you later Sarah," he said as he hurried from the room.

"This way Murdock." Sheriff Atkins spun around and strode toward his office.

"Apparently this guy's been missing for months," I began, after we'd settled into our chairs. "I'll do some checking, see if I can narrow down the last time anyone saw him and where."

Sheriff Atkins pulled out his yellow legal pad, flipped back the first two pages and jotted down some notes. "As soon as I hear from the guys in Redding, I'll e-mail you a copy of the autopsy report. I'm assuming you got some pictures."

"Yes sir, but I'd like some close-ups of the items he had in the canvas bag."

He scribbled one more thing on his pad. "I'll make sure that all gets sent to you."

"Also, I could use a copy of his DMV picture, in case folks don't know him by name."

"Check with Cindy. She can print you one." He flipped the pages back and set the pad off to the side. Then he picked up his receiver and started dialing.

"Thanks." I stood and moved toward the door. "I'll let you know what I find out."

Without looking up, he nodded and waved me away.

A few hours later, I'd finished my patrol and was pulling down my dark driveway. I parked next to the small barn, tossed Raven a flake of grass hay, and started toward the house. A piece of paper that had been tacked to the front door fluttered in the breeze. "Noticed you been gone all day. Got some dinner cooked at my place. Come on over." Remy! *Probably wants the scoop on the day's events, but if dinner is anything like his apple pie...* I turned on my heel, got into my truck, and drove straight to his place.

As soon as I stepped out of the Dooley, the smell of beef and vegetables had me drooling like Pavlov's dogs. After taking off my gun and stashing it under the front seat, I climbed the steps to the front door and knocked. I could hear the Highway Men singing inside and was just about to knock again when Remy opened the door. His red plaid shirt was unbuttoned and hung loosely over a white T-shirt; his black felt hat was nowhere in sight.

"Glad to see you took me up on my offer." He stepped back to let me in. "I've got some stew on the stove and I was just taking the bread out of the machine."

"Sure smells good," I said, following him into the kitchen. A red-checked tablecloth with matching curtains and seat covers decorated the small cozy room. A well-used, white enamel canister set with a red and black rooster on the front sat on the counter. A matching trivet, which read 'Peggy's Kitchen' hung over the stove.

Remy reached into the fridge and pulled out a bottle of Miller Genuine Draft. He twisted off the top and handed it to me. "This ought to keep you busy until I get the food on the table."

"Can I help?"

"Nope. Just sit yourself down. I'll shake out the bread and get it sliced." While I settled into one of the oak chairs, he pulled a small metal bucket out of the bread machine and turned it over onto a wooden cutting board. The loaf was golden brown and smelled heavenly; it made my stomach growled like a winter-starved wolf.

"This here contraption is the best dang invention. All I have to do is dump all the makings in, push a button, and in a couple of hours I got me a fresh-baked loaf of bread."

After slicing it and putting it on the table along with a cube of butter, Remy grabbed a cast iron pot off the stove and set it on a pad in the center of the oak table. "Dig in," he said, sitting across from me.

I ladled stew into my bowl and slathered butter onto a piece of bread. While I ate, Remy made idle conversation, telling me what he'd done that day and giving me the scoop about our mutual neighbors. When I'd emptied my bowl, he refilled it. "Now that you ain't starving, you can fill me in between bites."

I nodded but continued to chew. Sharing the facts of a case with unauthorized personnel is usually damaging to an investigation, but Remy might have information that could be useful.

"How much did you hear over the scanner?" I asked around a mouthful of stew.

"Just that there was a dead body near Upper Lake."

"Right. Hank and his boy, that's who found it, thought it might be some guy named Gus Miller."

"Gus Miller, huh? Thought he'd moved on."

"So did they. Apparently he hasn't been seen for a few months." I drained my beer.

"That's right. He used to be a regular at Pete's bar."

"Was he a friend of yours?"

"He wasn't a friend to nobody. Kept mostly to himself."

"Can you think of anyone who might know how he spent his days before disappearing?"

"Well, let me think." Remy stood, pulled two more beers out of the fridge, and offered me one. "There was Tom Lowry. He works over at the resort, and they'd sometimes come into the bar together."

"Resort? Around here?" I asked, opening my beer.

"Yep. High Desert Hot Springs. Been in business a long time. Caters to pilots of private planes who like to fly in."

"Really? I had no idea. Course it makes sense, what with all the geothermal water around here." I thought about my own bathhouse and how great a long soak would feel.

"Where does this Tom Lowry live?"

"From what I understand, right there at the resort."

I pushed my bowl away and pulled out my notebook. "Do you know where Gus lived?"

"His family had a homestead outside of Lake City. Most of the land's been sold off over the years except for the couple of acres where the house and barn sit."

"Did Gus have a vehicle?"

"Yeah, but it hasn't been around either. That's why most of us figured he'd moved on."

"What did he drive?"

"A 1962 Buick LeSabre. Sand colored with them chrome portholes in the front. Story goes he inherited it from his mother, but he drove that car everywhere, like it was a four-wheel-drive truck. Looked like it'd gone through a demolition derby."

"Well, that's kind of how Gus looked today." I leaned back in my chair to make breathing a little easier.

"What do you suppose killed him?"

"Don't know. I didn't see any bullet holes and there weren't any knives sticking out of him." Remy looked disappointed. "But it did look like he'd taken a blow to the head. I should know more after the autopsy report." I put away my notebook, drained my second beer and set the bottle down on the table. "What do you know about Indian artifacts around here?"

"Not much. There's a reservation here in Fort Bidwell so I guess there must be some in the area? Why?"

"Gus had a bag full of them."

"Don't that beat all. Wonder where he got them?"

"That was my next question. Any ideas?"

"Nope. It's no secret how Gus felt about them people, so I don't imagine any of them would tell him where to find those things."

"Looks like I'll need to have a look around Gus' place tomorrow and then talk with this Tom fellow."

"You want me to show you where the Miller place is? I don't mind."

"That's nice of you to offer, Remy, but I start my patrol pretty early."

"I'm up by five o'clock every morning. A habit I got working construction. That early enough?"

"Plenty. You'll probably save me some time trying to find it. Well," I said, getting to my feet, "I should be heading home. I need to write up my notes."

"Don't you want some dessert?"

"Remy, I don't know where I'd put it." I patted my bulging belly.

"Let me pack you up some. You can eat it later." He got up and pulled a paper plate out of the cupboard. Moving to the stove, he uncovered a flat square casserole and spooned out a generous helping.

"Looks good. What is it?"

"Apple Brown Betty."

"Betty who?"

"Apple Brown Betty. It's got sliced apples layered with

breadcrumbs and brown sugar. Peg used to make it all the time. I figured that if I ever wanted to enjoy it again, I'd have to learn how to make it. Only took me a few tries to get it right." He covered the plate with foil and handed it to me.

"Thanks." *Mmmm — breakfast.* "I'll pick you up around six-thirty."

"I'll be ready," Remy said, following me outside.

That evening, as I read through my notes, I wondered what I might find at Gus' place, what the autopsy report would say, and most of all, what the Indian artifacts had to do with this whole thing. Acting purely on a gut feeling, I dialed Sue's number and was about to hang up when a very sleepy voice came on the line. "You better be bleedin' or dyin'."

"Sue, it's me."

"Sarah? What time is it?"

"Nine-thirty my time, which makes it..."

"After midnight here. Is something wrong?"

"Sorry I woke you, but I need your help. I'm investigating this dead body I recovered..."

"Dead body! You told me nothing exciting ever happens in that place."

"It's not like he was killed by an ax murderer or something. In fact, I don't know how he died — yet. But that's not why I called. He had a bag full of stuff that I'm sure are Indian artifacts."

"Native American."

"What? Oh, right. Sorry."

"What exactly did you find?"

"Some bones with notches cut into them, a piece of deer antler, and obsidian. They were wrapped in a weaved mat of some kind."

"Can you send me pictures?"

"Soon as I get them. I'll also email you any other information I gather about the area, if you'll check for any illegal buying and selling of artifacts."

"You got it, but Sarah..." There was a pause. "There's something you need to know."

"What's that?"

"It's Hensley... he's gone."

"Yeah, I know. You already told me he got canned."

"No, that's not what I mean. It's like he's vanished. Even Morgan doesn't know where he is."

"Maybe he's just on a trip or something."

"Uh, uh. His clothes and other things are still in his condo, but his car's gone. No one has seen or heard from him for almost a week."

"So, what's this got to do with me?"

"Apparently he sent the deputy director an email, blaming you for the whole thing. Even called you the c-word. Said you saw it as an opportunity to get back at him for ending your relationship."

"But that was over a year ago."

"No kiddin.' That's what makes this whole thing so wacked."

"Well, thanks for telling me. Go back to sleep and I'll talk to you later." I hung up the phone and began typing everything I knew so far. When I'd finished my notes, I copied the information into an email and sent it to Sue. Then I stretched out in front of the television with a bottle of beer.

The lights in my rearview mirror are blinding. Where has this car come from? It gains on me with tremendous speed. I brace for impact, but it veers wildly to the left and rushes past me. I've seen the vehicle before but — Hensley! He speeds ahead until his taillights are pinpoints of red. Suddenly they are replaced by tiny headlights. Growing larger, I realize the car has spun around and is coming straight for me. I think of swerving off the road, but it's too dark to see what's out there. Closer and closer, the lights get brighter and brighter — my heart is pounding. I close my eyes and —

The blare of an air horn blasted me awake. Looking around and trying to get my bearings, I realized there was a high-speed chase on the television. A semi was trying to run an old sedan off the road as the two of them sped down a mountainside. The air horn cut loose again, just as I clicked the set off with the remote. Still feeling a little shaken, I shuffled into my room and climbed into bed.

Chapter 9

The moment I opened my eyes I knew I'd overslept. I should have been at Remy's ten minutes ago. *Damn snooze button.* I got dressed as quickly as I could and re-braided my hair on the way to the kitchen. A cup of microwaved instant coffee in one hand and a PopTart in the other, I dashed out the door, my gun belt swung over one shoulder.

"About time."

Tossing most of the contents of my cup down the front of my uniform, I spun around to find Remy resting comfortably in the Adirondack chair under my apple tree, his hat pushed back on his head. "You scared me to death!" I said, taking deep breaths to slow my pounding heart. "How'd you get here?"

"Walked. It's just a hoot and a holler from my house to here. Brought some fresh-brewed coffee and homemade banana muffins." He held up a large metal thermos and brown paper bag.

Without hesitating, I dumped out what was left in my cup and tossed the PopTart into the nearby garbage can.

As Remy got settled in the passenger's seat, I brushed off the splotches of spilt coffee and put on my gun belt. While I guided the Explorer up the driveway and toward the main road, Remy plopped a muffin on the dashboard in front of me and refilled my cup.

"So what's the plan when we get there?" Remy asked.

"No plan really. Just going to take a look around and try to figure out what Gus may have been up to."

"We gonna talk to Tom afterward?" He waited until we got to Fort Bidwell before handing over my cup.

We? "I don't want to take up your time. I'll be happy to take you home when we're done." The man frowned at me. "Of course, if you don't mind tagging along..."

"Not at all, not at all." He beamed. "Couldn't hurt to have backup."

Backup?

By the time we reached Lake City, I had gobbled down my muffin and finished off two cups of coffee. Remy tightened the lid on the thermos and slipped the bag of muffins under the seat. "Turn off here," he said, pointing to the right. "It's just about half-a-mile up this road."

Acres of green grass spread out on either side. Ranch houses surrounded by tall trees were strategically placed on the rolling fields, and huge barns, like sentinels, stood nearby. Next to the road, a small two-story building sat on a weedy patch of hardpan. Exposure to the elements had worn away all but a few flakes of white paint, leaving behind dull gray planks of old wood. An ancient elm tree had grown so close to the house some of its branches were resting on the roof. The first floor windows were hidden behind large sheets of old plywood.

"Who boarded up the place?" I asked as we got out of the Explorer.

"Must've been Gus. I can't think of another soul who'd be interested in this place."

"Really?" I moved to the back of the rig and pulled out my camera and a flashlight. "No other family in the area?"

"None that I know of. Like I said, he kept mostly to himself."

Stepping up on the small front porch, I saw that the

door had been secured with a lock and hasp. "Not a very trusting type either, I see."

"Maybe we'll have better luck with the back door," Remy suggested.

"Maybe." But the door at the back of the house was secured the same way. "Here, hold these for a minute," I said, thrusting the camera and flashlight into his hands. In a minute or two I returned with a small bolt cutter. One quick clip and the lock fell of the hasp. Shoving the door open, I was startled by the scattering of small furry creatures. "Rats!"

"What's a matter?" Remy asked.

"Rats. The place is full of them. Just a second." I pushed past him, returned to the front of the house, snapped the lock off that door, and flung it open. The scurrying and squeaking of so many creatures trying to avoid the sudden burst of light made my skin crawl. An overstuffed sofa and easy chair, with broken down seats, hunkered on the right side of the room, and a dining table covered with a thick layer of dust was on the other. A single chair with most of its pieces missing sat next to it, and cardboard boxes lined the wall. Directly in front of the door, a steep narrow stairway disappeared into the darkness of the second story.

Looking through the house, I could see Remy standing in the doorway, shaking his head. "Pretty nasty, wouldn't you say?"

As I looked around, I couldn't imagine anyone having lived there in years, let alone just a few months ago. I reached over and flicked the switch next to the front door but nothing happened. Unless I wanted to pry off the sheets of plywood, the search of the premises was going to be by flashlight. "See anything unusual in there?" I called to Remy.

"Nothing really, but I don't think Gus was planning on leaving the area."

"Why do you say that?" I crossed the room and stood in the doorway to the kitchen. The first thing I noticed was the smell, a combination of spoiled food and rodent urine. Almost every cupboard was opened and food had been scattered everywhere. Dirty dishes, growing some kind of fuzzy fungus, were piled in the sink. The once-white countertops were covered with dark splotches and the black rice-shaped feces of rodents. Crispy black banana peels were lying here and there, along with flattened, slimy green disks I assumed had once been oranges. I had to agree with Remy; Gus must have planned on coming home the day he disappeared.

"Wonder what he left in here?" Remy asked, moving toward the refrigerator.

"Freeze!" I yelled.

"What the hell!" So startled, he almost dropped my equipment.

"Sorry. I just didn't want you to open that," I said, pointing to the short, squatty refrigerator. "Trust me, anything left in there isn't important enough to chance opening it up. You gotta a hanky?"

"What for?" he asked, setting down the camera and flashlight. He pulled a blue and white handkerchief out of his back pocket.

"Tie it around your face, bandit style. No sense taking a chance on picking up a Hantavirus while we look around."

"A haunted what?"

"Hantavirus. It's a virus spread by rodents," I explained as I pulled an emergency mask out of a small compartment on my gun belt. "Let's make this quick and get out of here." Picking the flashlight up off the counter, I led the way up the stairs. Shadows danced across the walls as we made our way up the rickety steps. At the top were two doors, one on either side of the small landing.

"We'll try this one first," I said, stepping to the right and opening the door. The sudden burst of light made me want to scurry for cover like my furry friends downstairs. After my eyes were functioning again, I could see the long, narrow room was packed with pieces of old furniture and stacks of trunks. Everything was coated with a grimy layer of dust, and I could tell by the lack of tracks on the floor that no one had been inside the room for a long time.

"Seems old Gus didn't like to throw nothing away," Remy said.

"Let's see what's in the other room." I turned off the flashlight and stepped across the landing. The door hinges screeched in protest, making me appreciate the fact that I hadn't come alone. A heavy antique four-poster bed dominated the room. Dingy grey sheets were thrown back over a tattered patchwork quilt and a discolored impression decorated the pillow. The drawers of the gentlemen's dresser on the far wall were hanging open, and articles of clothing looked like they were trying to crawl out. The lamp on the small bedside stand consisted of an exposed bulb perched on a small brass base. The only other furniture in the room was a chair from the dining set with almost as many pieces missing as its twin downstairs.

"Wasn't much of a housekeeper either," Remy observed.

Walking to the other side of the bed, I spotted another quilt on the floor, more frayed than the first. "Did Gus have a dog?"

"Now that you mention it, I believe he did," Remy said, stepping further into the room. "Maybe Hank or some other neighbor knows where it is."

"Maybe so. We'll take another look around downstairs before we go see Tom."

"Suits me. This place is giving me the creeps."

You and me both.

At the bottom of the stairs, I turned to the left. I switched on the flashlight and opened the door. Even through the mask, the smell of stale urine was overwhelming. The tub, sink, and toilet were all infested with a black grunge of some kind, and chest-high stacks of newspapers lined the walls. Finding nothing significant to the case,

I stepped out and pulled the door closed. "Don't ask," I told Remy. "You don't want to know."

On the way to the kitchen, I remembered the boxes sitting on the other side of the dining table. "Wonder what's in these?"

Remy grabbed one of them and place it on the table. Odd-shaped rocks, worn by use, and pieces of obsidian were inside. "Let's see what's in the other two," I suggested. One had sections of woven mat like I'd found in the knapsack along with coned-shaped baskets. *More artifacts. This guy is... or rather was definitely up to something.* The third box contained bones and part of a human skull.

"Anybody you know?" I asked, nudging Remy in the arm.

"Let's get out of here," he said, taking off his felt hat and fanning himself with it. "I need some fresh air."

While my neighbor scooted through the kitchen, I shut the front door, grabbed my camera off the counter, and followed him.

"That's an experience I'd rather not repeat any time soon," he said, removing his handkerchief and mopping his brow with it.

I pulled off my mask and stuffed it into my front pocket. "I have to agree with you on that. Give me a minute to secure this place and we'll move on to our next stop." Grabbing a roll of duct tape, I re-entered the house, quickly sealed the boxes of artifacts, and stashed them in the back of the Explorer. I'd just finished securing the doors with a couple of extra locks I happened to have and stringing crime tape across both when Hank's red Dodge Ram drove up.

"Morning Deputy." He stepped down from his rig and strolled toward us. "Remy."

"Howdy, Hank."

"I see you've already been inside," Hank said, nodding at the dilapidated house. "Find anything?"

"Not much," I said before Remy had a chance to

answer. *Don't want to let out more information than necessary.* "I understand Gus may have had a dog."

"Yep. Never went anywhere without Chopper."

"Have you seen it around since Gus went missing?" I took out my notebook.

"No I haven't. Assumed it was with him."

"What kind of dog is it?"

"A blue heeler. Ornery old cuss, but he was a good cow dog in his day."

"Do you recall seeing anybody around here lately?"

"Can't say as I have."

"Call me if you see any suspicious activity." I pulled one of my business cards from the front flap of my notebook and handed it to him.

"Will do, Deputy." He slipped it into his shirt pocket.

"Thanks. Come on, Remy. Next stop, High Desert Hot Springs."

Chapter 10

"Looks more like a detention facility than a resort," I said, looking at the large two-story building. The fact that it was sitting on an endless alkali flat didn't make it look any more inviting.

"I hear tell it's something to see on the inside. Had one of them Olympic pools, but they filled it in to make a huge ballroom of some kind."

"Huh, I think I'd have kept the pool." I pulled off Highway 299 and parked next to a small fleet of older vehicles, all with the resort name and logo on the doors. Grabbing the manila folder with the scant information I had, I got out and started for the front door.

"Kinda feel like Dorothy in the land of Oz," Remy said, as we moved into the entryway. Huge ferns hung from the low ceiling, and brass furniture with off-white cushions and miniature palm trees lined both sides. Large prints of brightly colored flowers hung on the walls.

"I'm thinking more like Alice in Wonderland," I said, moving through the entry and further into the building. A huge room opened up off the entry, the high ceiling making it seem even larger. Small round tables with crisp linen cloths were clustered on one side; their wrought-iron chairs reminded me of open-air cafés in Paris.

"What do you mean?" Remy came up behind me.

I pointed to the other end where a gigantic chess set with two-foot pieces was positioned between an enormous stuffed chair and a giant big-screen television. The arrangement took up the entire wall.

"Well, now that gives a whole new meaning to 'supersize' don't it?"

Before I could agree, a very dainty woman burst through the pair of swinging doors mounted in the wall behind the tables. Her platinum-blond hair, piled high on her head, created an illusion of height for her short stature.

She halted a few feet away. "Can I help you?" she asked, her eyes moving from me to Remy and back again.

"Morning ma'am. I'm Deputy Murdock and I'm looking for Tom Lowry. I understand he works for you."

"That's right. He helps my husband with the maintenance and keeps the grounds cleaned up."

"Would it be possible for me to speak with him?"

"Is Tom in some kind of trouble?"

"No ma'am. I..."

"She's investigating a murder!" Remy blurted.

"Remy!"

"Sorry, sorry." He raised both hands and stepped back.

"Now ma'am..." I turned back to the tiny woman. Her wide eyes and white face reminded me of Billy Henrickson. "We're not sure how the man died, but I understand he was a friend of Tom's." I opened my folder and pulled out the copy of Gus' DMV photo. "Do you recognize him?" I held it out for her to see.

As she reached for the picture, some of her color returned. "Of course. That's Gus, but he hasn't been around for ages. I just assumed he and Tom had a falling out. You see, the last time he was here they had a big argument."

"An argument, huh?" I handed Remy the folder and pulled out my notebook. "And how long ago was that?"

"Oh my, before the big snow in January."

"Where would I find Tom?"

"I'm sorry but he's not here right now. He went to Alturas with my husband to pick up our new range." Her hazel eyes twinkled. "It's one of those big commercial ones for our remodeled kitchen — all stainless steel with a hood. They should be back in a couple hours. You could talk to him then."

"I'll try and stop by again sometime this afternoon. Thanks for your help, Mrs. ..."

"Flowers. Abigail Flowers. My husband, Ed, and I own the resort. His family has had it for many years, but when we took over, we decided to modernize it and give each room its own theme. I've had such fun locating and purchasing things for them. Must've hit every estates sale within two hundred and fifty miles."

"Is that where you found them things?" Remy asked, pointing to the Lewis Carroll style furniture.

I grimaced. *Good old Remy, straight to the point.*

"Why, yes!" She smiled at him. "They were at an auction in the central valley. Apparently the owners had some connection with the movie industry. I just love the way they look in this room, don't you?"

Remy glanced at me but didn't say anything.

"Thanks again," I said, ushering my companion toward the door.

A few minutes later we were back in the Explorer and heading north on County Road 1. I needed to get on with my patrol, but first I had to get Remy home. "I appreciate your help with..." The crackle of the radio interrupted me.

"113, this is Modoc."

I snagged the microphone from its hook on the dash. "Go ahead, Modoc."

"Sheriff wants you in Alturas ay-sap."

"What's going on?"

"Didn't say. Just wants you in his office right away."

"Copy that. Fasten your seatbelt, Remy," I said, replacing the mike. I increased my speed along the narrow road, taking advantage of the open stretches between ranches. It hadn't taken me long to discover that the ranchers considered the road to be part of their dooryards, and drivers had to be ready to dodge pedestrians as well as livestock.

An hour later, I'd turned over the boxes from Gus' house and was peering into the break room vending machine, waiting for the sheriff again. My stomach, held off temporarily by Remy's banana muffin, was demanding more. Wanting a healthy snack, I made my choice. As I retrieved my bag of trail mix, I heard voices coming from down the hall. Poking my head out the door, I saw Mayor Callaghan and the sheriff standing outside his office.

"Remember, Chet, elections are coming up this fall. If you want my continued support, you'll take care of this — quickly."

"Sure thing, Eugene. Right away."

When the mayor turned to leave, I slipped back inside and appeared to be reading the newspaper as he sped by. As soon as he rounded the corner, I hustled down the hallway and into the sheriff's office.

"Sit down, Murdock," he said. He finished writing something on his yellow legal pad before making eye contact with me. "Now, how much progress have you made on the Miller case?"

"I found some more artifacts when I searched the victim's house this morning. I've turned them over to Josh to be photographed and catalogued. His vehicle and dog are missing as well. I tried to contact an acquaintance, but he was not at his place of employment this morning."

"Here are your photos and the autopsy report," he said tossing a file across his desk, "but I'd like you to put this on hold for a while."

"Hold, sir?"

"There's a more pressing case I'd like you to investigate."

"What's that?" I asked, taking out my notebook.

"Apparently there's been a burglary at the Surprise Valley Convalescent Hospital. Mayor Callaghan's mother called him bright and early this morning. She believes someone has taken some jewelry — let me see..." he scanned over his notes, "...an heirloom necklace that belonged to her grandmother. As I'm sure you overheard, the mayor is pressuring me to get this resolved as quickly as possible and return the necklace." He tossed the pad aside. "I want you to go there and get a full description of it and have a look around. My guess is that it's just been misplaced and will turn up. Keep me in the loop on this one. If I know Eugene, he'll want hourly updates."

"Yes, sir. As soon as Josh is finished with the stuff from the Miller house, I'll go straight there."

"I'm counting on you, Murdock. Put that FBI training of yours to good use." He came around his desk and opened the door.

"Sure thing," I said, stepping into the hall and standing just about where the mayor had been. "I'll give you a call as soon as I know anything."

"I'd appreciate that." He moved back inside his office and closed the door.

Pressed for time, I hurried toward the lab. The contents of the boxes were spread out on the large viewing table, a small white tag attached to each one. The lab tech stood off to the right, next to a large photo printer.

"Boy, that's quite a set-up," I said, watching the pictures spit out, one after another. "I could sure use something like that."

"Didn't you get a smaller version of this when you started?" he asked, straightening the stack of photographs.

"No. All I have is an old 35mm camera that came in the investigation kit."

"We got digital cameras and photo printers for all of our deputies. Who issued your equipment?"

"The Undersheriff. What's his name?

"Sandusky?"

"Yeah, that's the guy."

"Wonder why he did that. He was the one that pushed to get the new technology in the first place."

"Well, can I get them today? It would sure save me time and trips over the mountain."

"Sure thing. Here's the inventory," he said, moving over to the table and passing over a handwritten list. Then he gathered up the photos and handing them to me. "Hang on a second and I'll be right back."

A few minutes later I had my new camera and photo printer loaded in the Explorer and was headed back to Surprise Valley. Before driving over Cedar Pass, I stopped at the local drive-in and ordered a double bacon-cheeseburger. Munching on my french fries, I wondered how long this new investigation was going to take. Maybe the sheriff was right; the necklace was just misplaced. The poor old lady probably had a hard time remembering her name.

As I parked in front of the convalescent hospital, I noted the layout of the building. Large windows ran across the front on either side of the entrance, which could allow access from the outside. The door and the panel next to it were made of glass, providing plenty of visibility.

Stepping through the door was reminiscent of my visit to the Silver Spur Saloon, eyes following my every move. Residents of the hospital lined both sides of the entryway, forming a geriatric gauntlet.

Before reaching the nurses' station, I was greeted by a slight man with horn-rimmed glasses and thinning hair. "Thank goodness you're here. Marjorie has been hounding me all morning."

"Marjorie?"

"Marjorie Callaghan. She's been demanding that we strip-search everyone. When I called the sheriff's office, they told me a deputy was on his way — I mean on her way. Sorry."

"Not a problem. Where is Mrs. Callaghan?"

"In her room. She refuses to leave it unguarded."

"I see. And you are?"

"Herb Leibowitz, hospital administrator."

"Well, Mr. Leibowitz, why don't you take me to her."

"Right this way." As he led me deeper into the building, the acrid smell of antiseptic and age assaulted my nose. When we stopped at a corner room in the front part of the building, I peered inside. The four beds were neatly made and each area had been decorated with family photos and mementos. An elderly woman dressed in a crimson velour running suit was seated directly in front of the door. Her steel gray hair was pulled back in a tight bun, making her angular features more severe. An aluminum cane rested across the arms of the chair.

"About time you got here, young woman. That'll be all Herbert." As she rose from her chair, Leibowitz scurried from the room.

"You must be Mrs. Callaghan," I said, extending my hand.

"Of course I am," she exclaimed, ignoring my gesture of greeting and shaking her cane at me instead. "Now, I want this facility, as well as everyone in it searched immediately. I want that necklace found."

"Yes, ma'am, but let me look around first. Are you certain the necklace hasn't been misplaced?"

"See here, I am not senile." She moved with a significant limp toward her bed. "I keep it right here in this jewelry box." She retrieved an ornate wooden box from the shelf above her bed, flipped the clasp and opened it. "As you can see, the necklace is no longer here."

I stepped closer to get a better look. Inside were some odd-looking coins, a skeleton key, and a tarnished spoon with "Chicago's World Fair" engraved on the handle. But no necklace.

"Can you describe the piece of jewelry for me?" I asked, taking out my notebook.

"Of course I can; it was my necklace!" She slammed the lid on the box and returned it to its place of honor, next to a framed picture of the mayor.

I'm beginning to understand why your son lives on the other side of the Warners!

"It was a rare cameo, larger than a silver dollar, carved from coral and mother-of-pearl. It is priceless, and I demand its return!"

"Yes, ma'am. I'll get started on the investigation right away. Do you mind if I look around your room?"

"You're wasting your time. I've already searched this room."

Slipping the notebook back in my pocket, I walked over to the window. After lifting the latch, I slid the pane over, but it only opened a few inches; a stop had been screwed into place, which prevented the window from opening all the way. I closed it and went in search of Leibowitz. I found him cowering down by the nurses' station.

"Excuse me, Mr. Leibowitz?" I said.

"Oh, please call me Herb." He pushed his glasses up with the index finger of his right hand.

"Okay, Herb. How many exits are there?"

His eyes shifted from me to the end of the hall and back. "Um, there are two. The front door and the rear door back by the kitchen."

"And are they left open all the time?"

"Only the front door can be opened from the outside, and it's locked at seven o'clock every evening. The back door is never unlocked. The crash bar allows people to leave the building but an alarm sounds if it's opened."

"What about the windows? I noticed the one in Mrs. Callaghan's room has a stop installed. Are all of them like that?"

"Yes. A few years ago we had a patient climb out one of the windows and went missing for several days."

"Mrs. Callaghan says she searched her room for the missing necklace."

"She sure did. Tore apart all the beds and dumped all the drawers. Fortunately her roommates were not in there at the time, and the nurses were able to get everything back where it belonged before any of them returned." As he spoke the last word, his eyes widened and what little color he had left his face. Turning, I wasn't surprised to find Marjorie Callaghan standing behind me.

"Thanks, Herb," I said, but when I turned back, he was gone.

Under the watchful eye of Mrs. Callaghan, I checked every window in the building and, after setting off the alarm to the back door myself, was convinced that the theft had to have been committed by someone who lived or worked in the hospital. The big question was who.

After I'd finished looking around, I found Herb cowering in his tiny office. "Has anyone else had anything stolen?"

"Why, I don't know. Marjorie is the only one who has reported anything missing."

I looked at my watch and was surprised to see that it was after four. "Okay. I'll be back tomorrow to interview the residents and look for any clues as to how the thief is getting away with this. What I need is a complete list of the residents, how long each has been living here, as well as a list of your employees."

"I'll have it ready for you. Anything else?"

"Not that I can think of right now. I'll see you tomorrow."

Exhausted from my visit with the mayor's mother, I let myself in the front door, lowered the bamboo blinds in the sun porch, and flicked on the computer. After putting the kettle on, I went back out to my patrol unit and brought in the camera equipment. Then I stepped into the bedroom and traded my uniform for fuzzy slippers and my Green Bay Packer's T-shirt.

Armed with a steaming mug of the chamomile tea that I'd bought on the way home, I sat at my computer to go over my notes and check my e-mail. Two messages came through. The first one was from Sue. Apparently there were two different groups connected to illegal activities involving artifacts, but only one of them had known dealings on the west coast. After opening the attachment, I downloaded the pictures it contained and printed them out on my new printer. I knew it was a long shot but figured maybe I'd get lucky.

The name on the other message sounded familiar, but I just couldn't figure out who it was — until I read it. Then I remembered Alexis was the name my sister had taken. Living in a condo in San Francisco, I'm sure she has major withdrawals unless she sees the inside of a mall at least four times a week. That's why her note made no sense; she was coming for a visit. She'd never bothered to visit me during the seven years I lived in Virginia, yet I'd been in Surprise Valley less than two months and she was announcing her arrival. It wasn't that I didn't want to see her — well, not entirely. I can tolerate her in small doses — in a crowded room — with loud music playing. But being alone with her for an extended length of time might possibly put me over the edge.

After staring at the screen for a few moments, I typed a quick reply: "Glad you're coming. It's been a while since we've spent some time together." Remembering my sister's knack for getting lost, and that Fort Bidwell wasn't exactly on the beaten path, I added: "Please go online for driving directions and a map." I hesitated, my finger poised over the mouse. I should tell her not to come, but instead I closed my eyes and pushed the button, sending the message into cyberspace.

Then I began the task of organizing the stuff I'd brought home. Using the bare wall of the sun porch as an evidence board, I sorted and put up the photos and itemized lists. Then I went over the autopsy report. Gus had sustained head trauma, possibly from some kind of rock. Based on the condition of the body, the coroner estimated his length of time underwater to be from two to four months. The odd thing was the water in his lungs. Could he have been alive when he went into the creek? If so, where was the primary crime scene? Figuring that out would have to wait. My priority, for now, was discovering who was stealing from the old folks' home.

Chapter 11

Getting an early start the next day, I'd just finished patrolling to the Nevada border when my cell phone rang. It was Cindy.

"What's up?" I asked.

"Some guy — Pete — wants you to stop by the Silver Spur Saloon when you get a chance. Nothing urgent he said, just needs to talk to you. Who is this guy? He sounds dreamy."

It was then that I understood why she had used the phone rather than the radio. "Oh I hauled away some guy who was throwing rocks at his trailer."

"Is he cute?" Poor Cindy. Being related to most of the single guys in town definitely was a disadvantage when it came to dating.

"I guess so," I said, thinking about his crystal-blue eyes.

"Well, maybe we should get together and have a drink at this Silver Spur Saloon.

"That sounds like a good plan, but I'm kind of tied up this weekend."

"Just so you know, I'm going to keep bugging you until I get to meet this guy."

"Understood. See you later." I disconnected and headed for the bar. Herb Leibowitz was expecting me, but there was no harm in postponing my visit a little longer.

Parking in front of the Silver Spur, I noticed there was

a maroon 1967 Pontiac GTO parked along the south side of the building. As I entered the dark interior, I pushed my sunglasses up onto my head. "Pete, are you in here?" I called.

A door at the back of the saloon opened and the tall bartender appeared. "Morning, deputy," he said, giving me a big grin. "Thanks for coming by." He came around the bar, pulled out a stool for me, and perched on the one next to it.

"Is that your car outside?"

"Sure is. Took me three years to restore her. I'll have to take you for a ride some time," he said, winking at me.

"Uh, did you need something?"

"I just wanted to thank you for stopping Bill the other night. Lucky for me, he was too drunk to aim, so I only lost one window."

"How did you know — Remy!"

"Yep. Stopped by the other afternoon and filled me in. Hope Bill wasn't too much of a pain for you, especially considering the way the two of you met."

"Not really. By the way, why didn't you want to press charges?"

"Bill tends to drink too much, and if he thinks you're out to get him, whether you are or not, he can get downright mean. Better to let him sleep it off and think you're afraid of him. Besides, that trailer is just a rental. Now if he was trashing my bar, that'd be different."

"But what about the damage he did with the stool?"

"All taken care of."

I glanced at the front of the bar. The gash Bill had left during his tantrum had been meticulously sanded and re-stained.

"So you own the place?"

"Yep. It was all boarded up when I bought it. Found most of this stuff," he waved his hand around, "in the basement. Been open five years now and doing pretty good. You'll have to come back some time when my band is playing. We're not all that great, but we're loud."

"Sounds like fun," I said, getting up to leave. "I should be going. Keeping the valley safe and all that." I started toward the exit.

"Right, right. And don't be a stranger." Pete followed me to door. "It's not often I get female customers, especially good-looking ones."

Good grief. As I pushed through the door, I could just hear Sue urging me to go for it, and Cindy saying to get out of her way. But I didn't have time for men at the moment; I had a date with Herb.

When I arrived at the convalescent hospital a little while later, several members of the greeting committee were missing. More pressing activities must have drawn them away. I went straight to Herb's office but was surprised to find it locked up tight. Figuring he was hiding from Marjorie again, I headed for the nurses' station. "I'm looking for Mr. Leibowitz," I told one of the nurses as I approached.

"I'm sorry, but he went home a little while ago. Poor man developed a migraine after Marjorie got through with him. But he did leave you this." She reached under the tall counter and pulled out a single piece of paper with a list of names scribbled on it.

"Thanks, I'll call him tomorrow." As I turned to leave, I spotted Marjorie Callaghan stumping her way up the hall. She hastened her step as soon as she saw me. When I moved toward the door, she hollered something at me, but I couldn't make it out. The last thing I wanted was another session with the tiny tyrant, so I did the only thing I could think of.

"Copy that Modoc," I said loudly into the radio mike clipped to my shoulder. "On my way." Practically running, I pushed through the double glass doors, jumped into my rig, and cranked the engine over. As I threw it into reverse, I flipped on the lights and siren and screamed out of the parking lot. It wasn't until I reached the city limits that I shut it all down and continued traveling north to finish off my day, patrolling that end of the valley.

By the end of the week, I was ready for a day off. I'd spoken to most of the clients at the convalescent hospital as well as the entire staff. No one had seen anything, so the burglaries must have taken place at night. A total of four residents had reported jewelry missing, but nothing else had been stolen since I'd begun investigating. However, the sheriff wanted answers and the mayor's mother continued to demand the return of her necklace.

Gus' case was just as baffling. What had happened, and where were his car and dog? Looking at a detailed map of the area, I traced Goose Creek to its origin at the base of Buck Mountain. The area, while only about ten miles from my house, did not appear to be very accessible by vehicle. However, on horseback I could reach the spot in a few hours. What better way to spend my day off, but first I needed a soak in the hot tub.

I stepped out into the crisp coolness of the morning and watched as the sun peeked over the ridge. The sound of birds filled the air. Hundreds, maybe thousands of them hid in the evergreen trees covering the slope behind my house. More of them flitted from branch to branch and tree to tree in the ancient cottonwood trees lining the creek. The grass sparkled under its drizzling of morning dew, and as I moved across it, the toes of my shoes drank up the moisture.

Feeling completely relaxed after my bath, I saddled up Raven, stashed a few supplies, and we trotted up the hillside. Occupied with a coast-to-coast move and the training to become a deputy, it had been several months since our last endurance competition. The creak of the saddle and the smell of the leather made me realize how much I'd missed it. There's nothing like moving as one with a large, powerful animal, riding cross-country, pushing yourself and your mount to the limits, and this ride would be no different.

The Warner Mountains are as unforgiving as they are beautiful. Steep ravines and sharp precipices are everywhere, and I made a mental note to get back before dark. Falling into one of those while wandering around in the blackness would be terminal, so I began setting markers on my GPS in order to retrace my steps on the trek home.

It took longer to get to Fandango Pass than I thought. Riding along the ridge tops was faster but often getting from one to another was a challenge. A large alpine meadow between the pass and Buck Mountain provided us with a place to rest and have something to eat.

By midday we'd reached the small peak and began the long descent to the start of Goose Creek. The area's watershed was enormous and very steep. Any amount of rain could fill the stream to capacity within a matter of minutes. I gave Raven his head and let him plot his own course over the flows of sharp volcanic rock.

Following the natural flow of the landscape, I came to a small ravine hidden by a grove of quaking aspen. The light breeze made the two-tone leaves sparkle in the sunlight like coins in a fountain. Weaving the horse through the white-barked trees and around a huge outcropping of weathered basalt, I was surprised to find an old car sitting on the other side. I dismounted and tied Raven to a small pine tree before taking a closer look at the vehicle. Even before I spotted the chrome portholes in the front fenders, I was pretty sure it belonged to Gus Miller.

Glad I'd brought the digital camera, I took several pictures of the car and surrounding area. A group of rocks had been arranged into a ring not far from the car, but the makeshift fire pit had nothing inside. No burned wood or ash. In fact, the entire area on either side of the creek looked like it had been swept clean with a huge broom. There were no stray limbs or piles of pine needles.

Looking around, I found nothing that resembled a

road. *How did he get that car in here?* With no tire tracks to follow, I began walking back and forth between the car and the edge of the creek, moving farther into the trees with each pass. Finally I came upon a dirt road not much wider than a train track. I took out my GPS, set another marker, and headed back to the old car. Because it was getting late and I'd have to start back soon, I decided to search the car on another day.

Speculating that Gus had been digging up artifacts somewhere in the area, I got out my binoculars and scanned the steep slope of the ravine. Across the creek I spotted a small cave about halfway up the incline, the mouth of it partially hidden by a stunted pine tree. Exchanging the field glasses for my Maglite, I crossed the creek and slowly made my way up the rockslide, careful not to lose my footing and go tumbling down to the bottom. After having one foot or the other slide out from under me a couple of times, I finally made it to the cave.

The low ceiling forced me to enter on my hands and knees, but within a few feet, the cave opened up enough I could stand. The air, permeated with a gamey smell, felt cool and damp. Olympia beer cans were scattered here and there, and there were several holes dug into the floor of the cave. Clear evidence that someone had been in there recently. An old kerosene lantern sat next to a box similar to the ones I'd taken out of Gus' house, but as I began rummaging around inside it, I heard a strange noise. Shining the beam of light further into the cave, I saw where it had come from. Or rather, what it had come from.

Curled up like a sleepy house cat, a mountain lion blinked back at me. Without taking my eyes off the animal, I switched the flashlight to my left hand and pulled out my Smith and Wesson .38 special. Smaller and lighter than my service pistol, it was more comfortable to wear in the shoulder holster under my Carhartt jacket. Also, its concealed hammer made accidental discharges less likely. *Now what?*

My mind flashed on a poster I'd seen in the break room. Published by the Department of Fish and Game, it offered tips on what to do, and what not to do, when encountering a mountain lion. The first suggestion was to maintain eye contact. No problem there! No way was I taking my eye off of the hundred pound kitty cat. Rule number two was not to run. Flexing my fingers around the grip of my pistol, I slowly began to back out of the cave. The huge cat made no move to follow me. Step by step I crept backward until my head bumped into the rock ceiling. No crouching had been the third rule, but I wasn't getting out of my predicament if I didn't. Watching the animal for any sign of movement, I placed one knee on the floor of the cave and then the other. Again I began backing out. As the opening closed down, I was forced to bend forward and support myself on my elbows, military style. When my knees felt the roughness of the volcanic rock, I knew I'd reached the mouth of the cave.

Moving as quickly as I could down the steep rocky slope, I made my way back to Raven. "Come on, fella," I said, grabbing his reins and shoving the flashlight back into the saddlebag. "Time to go." I threw my leg over his back and guided him toward the grove of aspens. Once we cleared the trees, I holstered my gun and we began the vertical climb back up Buck Mountain.

By the time we reached the top, we both were breathing hard, and Raven's neck was wet with lather. I pulled my binoculars out of the saddlebag and scanned the slope we'd just climbed. No sign of the mountain lion.

Wanting to put as much distance between us as possible, I urged my horse toward the first marker. This time when we reached the meadow, there was no resting. Instead I positioned myself over the front of the saddle. Taking his cue, Raven quickened his pace. One after another, we passed the markers I'd set, until finally, I could see the tops of the cottonwood trees that stood like sentinels along the creek.

By the time I'd turned the horse out into the pasture, the muscles in my shoulders and lower back were stiffening. But thoughts of ending my day the way it had begun faded quickly, for as I moved from the barn to the house, a bright red BMW Z3 screeched to a halt at the end of the driveway. It sped backwards and swung through the open gate. Only one person drove like that. With one more wistful glance at the bathhouse, I went to greet my sister.

The car skidded to a stop, the driver-side door opened, and a tiny dog bounced out and began sniffing around. Twin pink bows adorned its perky ears, and its rhinestone collar sparkled in the sunlight. Then Alexis shoved herself up out of the low-slung car. Her white miniskirt and sleeveless turtleneck were accented with a gold chain belt and matching earrings. As she struggled to keep her balance in a pair of white pumps with three-inch heels, I couldn't help wondering why this prima donna had come to this secluded corner of northeastern California.

"Sarah, darling," she called, waving her hand in the air. "I can't believe I'm finally here. It's been three hours since my last Starbucks latte. How can you stand being so far from life's necessities?"

"I find ways to cope. So how long must you — I mean, can you stay?"

"No more than a month..." she began, pushing her long, honey-colored hair back with her Ray-Bans...

A month!

"...and then I fly to New York to preview a new line of lingerie. Bubbles, come say hello to Auntie Sarah."

Good grief! "When did you get the mutt?"

"Bubbles is not a mutt." Alexis picked up the small dog and held it close to her face; its coat was the same color as her hair. "She's a Shorkie."

"A what?"

"A hybrid of Shi Tzu and Yorkshire Terrier."

"Uh huh. Would you like some help getting your stuff inside?"

"That'd be wonderful. Here precious," Alexis said, putting the dog down, "let Mommy get your things." She opened the trunk and pulled out matching pieces of Gucci luggage in various sizes, followed by a miniature red wardrobe trunk and matching round case, both decorated with tiny paw prints. "Bubbles and I had to travel light. There's not much room in this car."

"Uh huh." Picking up three of the smaller pieces, I started for the house. "I'll take these. Can you manage the big one?"

"Of course. I'm not helpless."

Returning for another load, it took all my self-control to keep a straight face. My sister, towing the huge suitcase on its built-in wheels, was attempting to negotiate the gravel driveway in shoes that had questionable stability on level ground. Every couple of steps or so, either she or the bag listed dangerously to one side. "Here," I said, grabbing the suitcase by the handle. "I'll take that. You get the red ones."

"Thanks, sis. You're a dear."

While Alexis set up housekeeping in the spare room, I heated up the leftover spaghetti I'd brought home from Remy's two nights ago. That and a bag of salad was the only decent food I had in the house. Just as I finished setting the table, my sister and her miniature mutt came into the kitchen.

"Is it okay if I put Bubbles' food here on the counter?" she asked, shoving a large ceramic canister next to the coffee maker.

"Uh yeah, sure. I guess so. Do you need something to put it in? I might have an empty whipped topping bowl in the cupboard."

"Oh no, I brought everything with me." Alexis hustled from the room and returned with an armload of stuff. A monogrammed mat went on the floor first, followed by the round piece of red luggage, which turned out to be portable dog dishes trimmed with huge rhinestones. She filled one side with dog food and the other with bottled water. "Come on Bubbles. Mommy has your dinner all ready for you." The tiny blond dog sniffed at the dishes, moved a few feet away, and lay down. "Oh, dear. You don't think she's ill, do you?"

"I'm sure the dog just needs some time to adjust to her new surroundings. Let's eat before it gets cold and then we can drink — I mean, have a drink while we visit."

"Terrific. I have so much to tell you."

Before I could get the pasta out of the microwave and onto the table, Alexis had vanished and reappeared, this time clutching three bottles of wine. "Where's your corkscrew?" she asked, setting the bottles on the counter.

"Don't have one."

"How do you uncork your wine?"

I tore open the bag of salad, dumped it into a bowl and pulled the plastic scissor-like tongs out the drawer. "If it doesn't have a screw top or come in a box, I haven't tried it."

"Not to worry." She left the kitchen again and returned with a small leather case. "What should we start with, a white or a red?" She unzipped the lid on the case and folded it back.

"Lydia..."

My sister frowned at me.

"Sorry — Alexis. If you want to discuss ale versus lager or how dark beer compares with light, I'm in. But as far as choosing one wine over another..." I shook my head as I dug the blue cheese dressing out of the fridge.

"Fine, I'll open the Pinot Noir. It'll go better with the meat sauce." She pulled a small flat piece of metal from the case and cut away the top of the foil cap. Using something resembling the hand press I'd seen my dad use to reload bullets, she removed the cork in two swift moves. "Wine glasses?"

Suppressing a chuckle, I scrounged two clear Solo cups from the cupboard. "Best I can do," I said, offering them to her.

Pressing her lips together, she took them and poured each of us a glass of wine. "Mmmm, sure smells good," she said as we sat down at the table. She spooned a small serving of spaghetti onto her plate and filled the rest of it with salad. "Do you have any flavored vinegar?"

"I don't have any vinegar," I said, filling my own plate in the exact opposite — small serving of salad and filling the rest with spaghetti.

"Lemon juice?"

I shook my head as I spun my fork in the mass of noodles and sauce.

"Then what am I supposed to put on my salad?"

Folding my lips around an enormous bite, I shoved the bottle of dressing toward my sister with my free hand.

Reluctantly, she poured a small amount onto her plate and proceeded to moisten her fork in it before stabbing it into the lettuce. A technique I was certain Sue never thought of.

I washed down the spaghetti with a big gulp of wine. "Hmm, this stuff isn't bad."

Alexis took a sip from her own glass. "Most people don't chug fine wine."

"I'll keep that in mind. So, what made you decide to come for a visit?"

"Actually, I've come for two reasons. I don't know if Mom told you — a couple of months ago I became the senior assistant to the Northwest Buyer for Nordstrom's. Well, she's hoping to get promoted to National Merchandise Buyer, and if I can convince her I'm indispensable, she's sure to make me her assistant. Do you know what that could mean?"

"Uh uh," I said, as I helped myself to the last of the spaghetti.

"Travel, fashion shows, maybe even a designer show."

"Thaf sumbs gref," I said, my mouth full of food. I swallowed. "But what's that got to do with coming here?"

"Research. I have this marketing idea, but first I have to do some research."

"Uh huh — and the other reason you're here?"

She pushed her salad around on her plate. "That's a little more personal."

I waited for her to go on. When she didn't, I changed the subject. Or thought I did. "How is…" My mind was a blank. What was her boyfriend's name? Silver and stainless steel popped into my head, but I knew that wasn't right.

"Sterling?"

Sterling, of course. I knew it had something to do with silverware. "Yeah, how is Sterling?"

"I told you it was personal, and I don't want to talk about it." She guzzled her wine, shoved her chair back and stood. "If you'll excuse me, I'd like to go lie down. Bubbles, come!" The little dog got to her feet and trotted after her master.

I poured myself another glass of wine and began to clear the table. By the time I had the mess cleaned up, the wine was gone, and I didn't care that my sister was in her room sulking. I had one more day off, so I was going to enjoy my evening — alone!

After grabbing a beer out of the fridge, I stretched out on the sofa and began surfing the channels.

Chapter 12

Laying my head on the kitchen table, I listened to the gurgle of the coffee maker. My pounding headache had subsided to a dull pain behind my left eye. I should have known better than to mix wine with beer — several beers. On top of that, it took forever for my sister to fall asleep, and the sofa bed squeaked every time she changed position.

I had just closed my eyes, determined to prolong the quiet of morning when I felt something brush my foot. Peering under the table I found myself face-to-face with a dust mop dressed in a pink satin robe and four matching bunny slippers. What people do with their pets is their own business, but I was pretty sure that what my sister was doing to this dog was just plain cruel.

"Unbelievable!"

"What's that?" Alexis said, stumbling into the kitchen. She was dressed in an identical outfit with the exception of a pink satin sleep mask, which was shoved up on the top of her head. Her hair, so meticulously arranged the day before was a frizzy, tangled mess, and the dark circles under her brown eyes gave her a haggard appearance. "How can you sleep here? It's way too quiet."

Too quiet? How can it be too quiet? "How about some coffee?" I asked, getting up and moving over to the counter.

"That would be great," she said, sliding into the other chair. "Is it Sumatra or Columbia?"

"Ugh, neither. They're too bitter. It's Folgers."

Alexis crinkled up her nose. "Well, I guess I *am* roughing it." I rolled my eyes as I filled two mugs and carried them over to the table. My sister pulled one closer and warily smelled the black liquid. "You wouldn't by any chance have some flavored creamer, would you?"

"Nope. There's milk in the fridge and sugar in the bowl." I nodded toward the center of the table.

Giving me a thin-lipped smile, she took a tiny sip. "So what do you have planned for today?" she asked, setting her cup down.

"Well, I thought we might take a ride up into the Warner Mountains. There's a quick chore I need to do, and then we can go sightseeing if you'd like."

"What about breakfast?"

"We can grab something at the café in Cedarville."

"Breakfast in a quaint little café. How delightful!"

Quaint isn't exactly how I'd describe the Wagon Wheel. "How long until you're ready to go?"

"No more than an hour. It's just a road trip, right?"

"Well, that'll give me time to do a few things."

"Come on, Bubbles," Alexis cooed. "Let's get ready." She bustled out of the kitchen with her canine clone close behind. "Auntie Sarah's going to take us on an adventure. Yes, she is — yes, she is."

Give me a break.

Forty-five minutes later, I'd gotten dressed, fed Raven, gone back over my notes for both ongoing investigations, and was pacing back and forth across the driveway. I'd decided to take the Explorer because I wasn't so sure I could get my diesel truck down the narrow road and turned around. Plus I'd have everything I needed to gather any evidence I might find.

Finally my guests came strolling out the front door. Alexis was dressed in a pair of jeans that fit like a second skin, a low-cut blouse, and a long, brown suede coat with matching boots that reached to her knees. Her long blond hair, parted in the middle, had that just-brushed-back look it takes hours to achieve. "All set," she called, patting the gigantic bag she had slung over her shoulder. It was black with pink and white polka dots, and I shuddered to think what she had inside. Not to be left out of the fashion spotlight, Bubbles had on a denim jacket and cowboy boots — four of them.

"We'll be going in the Explorer, so the dog can ride in the back."

"Just a sec." Alexis opened the passenger side of her small car and unhooked some kind of cloth basket. Carrying it over to my vehicle, she installed it in the back seat and plopped Bubbles inside. "There, now you can see out the window," she told the dog. Then she climbed in the front seat and buckled her seatbelt. Shaking my head, I angled in behind the wheel, and we were on our way.

We reached the Wagon Wheel thirty minutes later, and after a brief discussion about the appropriateness of taking a dog to breakfast, I escorted my sister inside.

"Oh my, this isn't exactly what I'd expected," she said, looking around.

"How's that?" I led the way to a booth in the corner where the waitress met us with menus and water.

"Well, where's the cozy little tables with mismatched chairs, the hanging pots of herbs, the rustic wood paneling? This place is just so..."

"Retro?"

"Well, hmm... No, that's not it. It's so

"Yes?"

Alexis crinkled up her nose. "Pink and green."

"Well, I like it." I signaled the waitress to let her know we were ready. Sal, short for Sally, wasn't a day over sixty and had brassy blond hair, which she wore piled on her head. I'd quickly become one of the café's regulars and enjoyed chatting with her. My only complaint was that she often helped herself to my french fries while the plate was in transit. "I'll have the usual," I told her when she arrived at our table.

"Got it. Dry wheat toast and coffee. And what about you Hon?"

"Don't you have any croissants?" Alexis asked, scanning the menu.

"It's not that kind of café," I told her.

"Organic pancakes?"

"Not that kind of café."

"Rye toast?"

I glanced up at Sal. She shook her head. "Cookie does put out a nice bowl of oatmeal," she offered. "It really sticks to your ribs."

Alexis glared at the waitress and then turned her icy stare on me. "Dry wheat toast and herb tea."

"Uh, ma'am..." Sal began.

"I know, don't tell me — no herb tea. Lipton, do you have Lipton?"

"Yes ma'am, we sure do."

"Fine." Alexis relinquished her menu. "Dry wheat toast and a cup of Lipton. Lunch better come early," she hissed at me when Sal had moved back to the counter.

"You have to admit it does have a nice atmosphere."

"Atmosphere, schmatmosphere. I'm starving. Just where are we going anyway?"

Anxious to change the subject, I explained to my sister about needing to find the road to Gus' car.

"What if we get lost?" Alexis asked.

"Don't worry, we won't. I have my GPS unit and a detailed map of the area. We should be able to drive right to the place."

But things rarely, if ever, go the way you plan. After two hours of bumpy road and hysterical screaming about the bumpy road, I was ready to get out of my rig and walk off into the Warners, never to be seen again. The third time we backtracked, however, I managed to reach the GPS marker I'd set on the narrow dirt road the day before.

"What are you doing?" Alexis screamed, as I pulled off

the road and began maneuvering between the trees. She grabbed the dashboard as if bracing for a collision.

"Relax," I said. "I'm just going to park up here. We can walk the rest of the way."

"Walk? Are you crazy?"

"It's just through those trees. You can wait here if you want, but I'm not sure how long this will take." I turned off the engine, climbed out, and grabbed my silver evidence case out of the back of the Explorer. As I made my way toward the old Buick, I could hear Alexis babbling to her mutt as she got out of the rig.

After opening my case on a large, flat boulder, I slipped on a pair of latex gloves and stepped over to Gus' car. I took hold of the door handle, pushed in the large chrome button and gave the door a good yank. It wrenched open, the hinges shrieking in pain. Stale, musty air flowed out.

The inside was strangely devoid of the usual cast-offs of daily living that vehicles tend to collect. The threadbare carpet on the floorboards was covered with a fine layer of silt, almost as if a sandbag had leaked its contents. A set of keys hung from the ignition, making me more certain than ever that whatever happened to Gus happened close by. But why not get rid of the car? Perhaps the assailant, if there was one, knew it would be hard to find.

I grabbed the keys, got out, and moved to the back of the vehicle. Just as I put the key in the slot, I heard my sister approaching. Her knee-hi boots had large, clunky heels and she struggled to keep her balance. The large bag she had on her shoulder didn't help; if anything, it tipped her from one side to the other.

"Ooh, it's so dusty up here," she said, brushing herself off and dabbing at her face with a white lacy handkerchief.

"I thought you were going to wait in the car."

"I wanted to see you in action. What are we looking for?"

We? "I'm looking for anything that might tell me how the owner of this car died."

"Do you think he was murdered?" she whispered.

"Why are you whispering?" I asked, using the same hushed tone.

"You know, in case the killer is still around."

I laughed. "Alexis, the guy was killed a few months ago."

"Oh... oh!" she said. "Then I guess it's safe for Bubbles to look around."

"Where is the mutt?"

"Right here," Alexis said, patting the huge bag. As if on cue, the small dog poked her head out of one side. My sister retrieved the Shorkie and set her on the ground.

"Keep an eye on her," I said, thinking the petite pooch would make it a tasty snack for the mountain lion I'd found in the cave the day before.

Leaving my sister to make herself comfortable on a nearby rock, I turned the key and popped the latch. Lifting the lid of the trunk, I was surprised to find an odd collection of items inside. An old dented toolbox, a rusty can of gas, a couple quarts of motor oil, and an antique pickax occupied one side. The spare tire sat in the middle of the trunk, and an opened bag of Old Roy dog food, the discarded container of a Hormel canned ham, and a filthy gallon jug half-full of what I assumed was water sat on top of it. The other side held a small stack of newspapers, a dirty coil of cotton rope, and two empty boxes. Crammed in front of the spare tire were an old, metal Coke-a-Cola cooler and an opened can of coffee. After closely examining everything and making a detailed inventory of the trunk, I still had no clue what had happened to Gus or his dog.

As I slammed the lid and leaned on the back of the car, a strange noise came from underneath. Getting on my hands and knees, I looked for the source of the sound. A tangle of branches, leaves, and pine needles were packed tightly together, and Bubbles had wiggled into part of it. She was growling, trying to get at something inside the twisted mess. Cursing at the dumb dog, I hunkered down lower and began crawling under the Buick. That's when I noticed the rope. Similar to the one in the trunk, it was tied to the back bumper and ended somewhere amid the pile of branches.

I reached out, took hold of the rope, and slowly began pulling it toward me. As I did, part of the mess came with it, closely followed by Bubbles who was still pawing at something.

When everything cleared the back of the car, Alexis who had noticed the commotion, quickly picked up her dog. "Bad girl, Bubbles. You should stay where Mommy can see you. Whatever was she making such a fuss over?" she asked, leaning down closer to get a better look.

"Beats me," I said. Slowly I began to pull away the debris in order to see what was attached to the end of the rope. As soon as I realized it was the skeleton of a dog, I heard my sister gasp.

"Oh, my it's a — it's a — Bubbles, don't look!" She placed her hand over the dog's eyes and hurried back toward the Explorer. Chuckling to myself, I bagged the dog's remains and continued my search.

How did all that debris get piled under the car? And what killed the dog? Starvation? Dehydration? Again I looked around. Clean swept banks of the creek, an empty fire pit; I began to realize what might have happened. But to be sure, I'd have to look downstream.

Grabbing a large, black garbage bag from my kit, I began moving along the creek bed. Thick stands of willows grew on both sides. As I rounded the first bend, I spotted some kind of a wooden frame half-buried next to a large boulder. Pulling it free I saw that it was a screen from the window of a house. I leaned it against the large rock and continued looking. By the time I'd gone a half-mile, I'd recovered an old coffee pot, another empty canned ham container, part of a shovel, and an old army blanket.

When I got back to the Buick, I crammed the stuff I'd collected into the backseat. A quick phone call in the morning would get the vehicle towed back to the sheriff's office where Josh could give it a good going-over. However, the artifacts I'd discovered in the cave needed to be secured right away. I just hoped the feline resident wasn't at home.

Climbing part way up the rocky hillside, I chucked a good-sized rock into the cave and waited. When nothing happened, I threw in one more just to be sure. Still no sound or movement came out of the cave; it had to be empty. I climbed the rest of the way and crawled inside. Using the miniature LED flashlight on my key ring, I located the box and dragged it to the entrance. After sliding back down the hill, I stopped at Gus' car just long enough to grab my evidence case and the bag that contained what was left of his dog. Then I headed back to the Explorer.

"Finally!" Alexis declared when I opened up the back. "Can we go now? I've had all the wilderness I can handle for one day." Her seat was reclined, and she was holding a small water bottle to her forehead.

"Sure thing. Let me get this stuff loaded and we'll get going."

My sister popped her seat to the upright position and craned her neck to get a better look. "What is all that?"

"Just some artifacts and Chopper."

"Chopper?"

"The dog." I slammed the cargo door and slid in behind the wheel.

"Dog? What — you mean the — ooh, I think I'm going to be sick!" She spun around, dropped down the back of her seat, and reapplied the water bottle to her head.

As soon as we got back to my house, Alexis rushed to her room, lit a "calm" aromatherapy candle, pushed in her "Sounds of the Ocean" CD, and collapsed onto the bed. While she was recuperating, I grabbed a beer and sat at my desk. I needed to check my email, and there was a message on my answering machine. Hitting the playback button, I immediately recognized the voice; it was Herb Leibowitz. There'd been another robbery at the Surprise Valley Convalescent Hospital.

Chapter 13

After checking my notes, I punched in the number to the convalescent hospital. "Herb Leibowitz," I requested when the call went through. Several minutes passed before he came on the line.

"This is Mr. Leibowitz."

"Hi Herb, Deputy Murdock."

"Oh, deputy I'm so glad to hear from you. Marjorie's got the residents worked up and I could really use your help."

"Well, actually I wasn't planning to stop by until tomorrow. You see, it's supposed to be my..."

"But you have to come right away. She's got them in the dining room and has convinced some of them not to return to their rooms until the entire place is searched. The rest are protesting the search."

"Calm down, Herb." I checked my watch; it was just after one. "I'll be there around two o'clock and see what I can do."

"Thank you."

"Give me the name of the most recent victim."

"Clara Walsh. She discovered her pin was missing this morning. She's been very understanding — so unlike Marjorie."

"Okay. Don't let anyone leave the facility until I get there."

"Of course, whatever you want."

I hung up, shoved my beer back in the fridge, and

went to tell my sister I was leaving. "Lydia — I mean, Alexis," I called through the closed door of the guest room. "I have to go take care of something. I shouldn't be gone too long." When there was no answer, I opened the door. My sister was supine on the sofa bed, her pink satin sleep mask over her eyes, and the sound of ocean waves vibrating off the walls.

"Did you hear me?" I asked. "I need to talk to some people at the convalescent hospital and I shouldn't..."

"Convalescent hospital?" She ripped the mask off her face and sat straight up.

"Yeah, and I won't be too long..."

"Perfect!" She leaped from the bed and snapped off the CD player. "Perfect, perfect, perfect. Just give me a second to gather some things and I'll be ready."

"Ready for what?"

"Why, to go with you of course!"

"Won't you be more comfortable staying here? I don't know how long this will take and I don't want..."

"Don't worry about me. I've got some field research to do and this will be perfect."

"So you've said." I frowned at my sister. "What are you talking about?"

"These!" She pulled one of the matching pieces of the Gucci luggage out of the closet and held it open.

"Those look like..."

"Slippers! It's our new line and I brought them to try out."

"Try out?"

"You know, get people's opinion. I'm experimenting with this new marketing approach and if it's successful it could mean a promotion." Her brown eyes gleamed.

"I don't think so. This is official business and you'd just..." Then it came to me. Perhaps Alexis and her slippers would keep the residents, including Marjorie Callahan, occupied long enough for me to look around. "Fine, you can come but I'm leaving in ten minutes. You hear me, ten minutes."

"Okay, okay. I just need to get Bubbles changed.

"Changed?"

"Yes. She can't go out looking like this." Alexis lifted something that resembled a rolled-up towel off the bed. Taking a closer look, I realized it was the tiny dog, dressed in a white terrycloth robe, complete with hood.

"For the love of ... whatever! Just don't keep me waiting." I left my sister bustling around like a squirrel on speed and went to change my own clothes. Ten minutes later the three of us were on the road to Cedarville.

"So what have the old folks done to get you on the job?" Alexis asked.

"Someone is stealing from the residents."

"What are they taking?" she giggled. "Dentures?"

This is a mistake! "Come on, Alexis. Most of these people have only a handful of possessions to remind them of the life they used to have." I glanced at my sister. "And now even those are disappearing at the hands of a thief, so don't sit there and..."

"Okay, you win. Forget I said anything."

If only it were that easy.

Arriving at the convalescent hospital a few minutes later, I was surprised to find the entrance void of its usual occupants. "Boy, Leibowitz wasn't kidding," I said as we moved further into the building.

"Kidding about... eeww, what's that smell?" Alexis crinkled her nose.

"Don't even start." I flashed the look of death at her and kept moving. Just as we reached the large room that served as the dining hall, I pulled her aside. "Stay here. I'll get my interview done as quickly as I can." I took a few steps and then turned around. "And try not to be too much of a pain."

"Me, a pain? Are you kidding me?"

I shook my head and went in search of the mild-mannered hospital administrator. Playing a hunch, I found him at the nurses' station, trying to look invisible.

"You're here!" he exclaimed, jumping to his feet. "Will you help me get them back to their rooms?" He started back the way I'd come.

"Just a minute, Herb. I'd like to interview Mrs. Walsh first and maybe have a look around."

He paused for a moment, shifting his gaze from the direction of the dining hall to me. "Of course, of course. This way." He moved past me and started down the hall. We stopped a couple doors down from Marjorie's room. He tapped on the door, and without waiting for a reply, opened it, and we stepped inside.

"Clara," he began, "this is Deputy Murdock."

"Good afternoon, Mrs. Walsh," I said to the rather delicate-looking woman reclining in the hospital bed. "If you don't mind, I'd like to ask you a few questions."

"Certainly, sweetie. Sit down," she said, motioning to the chair next to her bed.

Leaving Herb to stand guard at the door, I pulled out my notebook and made myself as comfortable as possible in the metal folding chair. The petite patient reminded me of my own grandmother. Fine white hair sat on her head like huge cotton balls. Her lipstick was bright red and the apples of her cheeks were dotted with rouge. She looked like she belonged at a Sunday Social rather than in a hospital bed.

"What was taken and when did you notice it was missing?"

"My mother's brooch. I looked for it yesterday because my grandson was coming for his monthly visit. He's so busy you know."

"Yes, ma'am. When was the last time you saw it?"

"Last month."

"Are you sure you haven't misplaced it?" I asked, looking at the stark room.

"Oh, yes. I keep it right here." She opened the drawer of the nightstand and pulled out a small leather box. Using every ounce of strength she had, she lifted the spring-hinged lid. A small piece of red velvet was the only thing inside. "It's beautiful," she said, her deep blue eyes filling with tears. "A large black snowflake with a lovely blue sapphire set in the middle."

"Had you shown it to anyone since you wore it last?"

The old lady shook her head as she snapped the lid shut. Then her eyes widened. "Oh my, I forgot I'd shown it to Mary a few days after she arrived."

"Who's Mary?"

"Our newest resident," Herb offered.

"Yes, she's one of the lucky ones."

"Lucky ones?" I asked.

"Her son, Lucius, comes to see her once a week. Such a nice man." She leaned toward me. "You see, his mother is confined to a wheelchair," she whispered. "He is so thoughtful, always takes her for long walks every time he visits."

"I see. Where is Mary now?"

"Oh I'm sure she's with the others. Since I twisted my ankle, these people," she waved her hand at Leibowitz, "won't let me out of bed for another week."

The man gave her one of his weak grins.

"Thank you Mrs. Walsh," I said, getting to my feet. "I'll let you know if I find out anything about your pin."

"Thank you, sweetie."

Stepping out into the hallway, I could hear a commotion coming from the direction of the dining hall. Herb and I exchanged glances and hurried toward the noise.

When we walked into the large room, I thought the hospital administrator was going to have kittens. All the color left his face and small beads of sweat erupted across his expanding forehead. Almost every resident had on a fancy slipper from Nordstrom's, and a blue-haired woman was cooing at my sister's dog dressed in its pink hat and scarf with matching tennis shoes — four of them. Marjorie Callaghan stumped back and forth in front of the doorway, a searing look on her face. In the middle of it all stood Alexis, waving a black velvet slipper with a white rose attached to the toe. She was speaking to a redheaded woman seated in a wheelchair.

"But ma'am... what is your name?"

"Mary. Mary Littlefield and I told you, I am not interested in putting on any of your slippers."

"Please try it, just for a second. It's much more comfortable than the shoes you have on now. I mean how can these old worn-out shoes keep your feet warm. The holes in the bottoms of your soles must let in cold air. Here let me have one of them, so you can try this slipper on for size."

"NO!" But before she could do anything, Alexis whipped off her shoe and crammed the slipper onto her foot. "See there. Look how nicely that fits. Isn't that more comfortable?"

"Give me back my shoe this instant!" the woman shrieked, half-rising out of her wheelchair.

"Just a moment, ma'am," I said, hoping to defuse the situation. "Let me get that for you." Glaring at my sister, I snatched the old tennis shoe out of her hand. As I did, Clara's pin clattered to the floor.

Without warning, Mary leaped out of her wheelchair and dashed toward the exit. She was remarkably quick for her age, but she was no match for Marjorie. As Mary tried to pass through the door, the mayor's mother stuck her cane between the poor woman's legs and sent her flying. "Herbert," she called, waving her cane at the nervous man. "Call the police!"

"But..." Leibowitz looked in my direction, a look of uncertainty on his face.

"It's all right, Mrs. Callaghan," I said. "I'll take care of this."

"Well then, snap to it. And..."

"I know. You want your necklace back." I approached the surprised woman sprawled on the floor. "Mrs. Littlefield, I'm going to have to ask you to come with me." Gasping for breath, the woman got to her feet and looked at Marjorie. "Just get me away from that crazy woman," she said, pointing at the cane-wielding Mrs. Callaghan.

"Yes ma'am. This way." As I led the geriatric jewel thief toward the entrance, I called over my shoulder, "Alexis, you have five minutes to get that stuff gathered up and get in the vehicle or I'll have to come back for you."

"Be right there," she said, snatching slippers off feet as fast as she could. She had them and Bubbles stuffed back into their appropriate bags before I had my prisoner secured in the back of the Explorer.

"Glad to see you got this case solved so quickly, Murdock," Sheriff Atkins said when I briefed him back at the office.

"When Mrs. Littlefield told me about their scam, I contacted the guy at the pawn shop. Apparently he still has most of the jewelry. We've put out an APB for her son, and Deputy Jenkins is checking out the guy's house. But in all honesty, if it hadn't been for my sister, I don't think I would have figured it out so quickly."

"Well, I'd like to meet this sister of yours. Maybe we could use her on the force."

"Uh, maybe." I excused myself and retrieved my sister from the front lobby. "Sheriff, this is my sister Alexis. Alexis, Sheriff Chet Atkins."

"Really? I used to listen to your records when I'd visit our grandmother. You certainly have aged well."

The sheriff's face turned crimson. Without a word, he spun on his heel and stomped off toward his office.

"What on earth was that about?" Alexis asked.

"That's not *the* Chet Atkins."

"It's not."

"Of course not. And he doesn't appreciate it when people make references to that effect. In fact he usually assigns some kind of disgusting duty to those who do." *And I hate to think about which one I'm going to get.*

Chapter 14

My head was pounding before we'd reach the summit of Cedar Pass. My day off had died an ugly death, Alexis had irritated the sheriff, and there was nothing good to eat in the house. With any luck Morrison's Mercantile in Cedarville would still be open when we drove through.

"My, this certainly was a busy day. Are all your days off this hectic?" Alexis asked, checking her make-up in the visor mirror.

A sharp pain shot through my left eye, and I could feel the muscles in my shoulders bunching. "No!"

"Well, what do you have on the agenda for tomorrow, and when do we eat? I'm starving!"

"I'm hoping the store in Cedarville is open," I said through clenched teeth. "Otherwise it's peanut butter sandwiches and beer."

"Peanut butter! Are you kidding me? I can't eat peanut butter. I'm on this special low fat diet. Is the beer light beer? Do you know how many calories are in ...?"

"Alexis! Stop! Just sit there quietly; you're giving me a headache." I massaged my right temple.

"Poor Auntie Sarah," Alexis whispered to the miniature mutt in the backseat. "She has a headache, yes she does."

I yanked the wheel to the right and swerved off the road. "Look here," I hissed after bringing the vehicle to an abrupt stop. "If you don't sit there quietly until we get home, I'm going to take you up into the Warners and leave you there. Do you understand?"

Alexis, her eyes as big as donuts, nodded, eased back into her seat and looked straight ahead. Guiding the Explorer back onto the road, I took a deep breath and forced my neck and shoulders to relax.

It was beginning to get dark by the time we left the mountainous road and pulled into Cedarville. The small store was closed up tight, and we were out of options for dinner. The thirty-minute ride back to the house seemed unbearably long. Even Bubbles began to whine before we got there.

"She has to go potty," Alexis said softly.

"What?"

"She has to pee," she said, a little louder.

"Can't she wait until we get home?" I asked, glancing back at the tiny dog.

"She only whines when it's urgent."

"Damn." I pulled over and slammed the rig into park. Alexis jumped out, pulled her dog out of the basket in the backseat and set her down in the tall weeds by the side of the road.

As I waited for Bubbles to take care of business, I fought the urge to drive off and leave the pair behind. Finally the two of them were back inside, and we were on our way again.

By the time I pulled into the driveway, I was ready to forgo the peanut butter sandwich and just have beer for dinner. After parking the Explorer, I got out and headed for the front door, leaving Alexis to collect her junk.

Tacked in the usual spot was a note from Remy, inviting both of us to dinner. I let myself in and pulled off my uniform. As I slipped into a pair of sweats and a T-shirt, I yelled to Alexis, "If you want something to eat, I'm going to Remy's for dinner. Now!"

"Who's Remy?" she asked, stumbling in under her load.

"My neighbor. I'll explain on the way — if you get ready fast enough." I ran a brush through my hair and slipped on a pair of running shoes.

"Do I have time to freshen up?"

"No!"

"Can I at least change Bubbles?"

"Absolutely not! I'm going right now!"

"But... "

"Right now! You want to eat, get in my truck."

Alexis dashed into the guest room. In less than a minute she was at the door with Bubbles tucked under her arm, minus her hat and shoes.

"For Pete's sake, can't you leave that damn dog home?"

"I told you, she goes everywhere with me. Besides, if I leave her home alone, she tends to chew things up."

"Well, then by all means, bring her along," I said, opening the door and waving the two of them through. Within a few minutes, I was knocking at Remy's.

"Well, you look like you've had quite a day," he said when he opened the door.

"You don't know the half of it. Remy, this is my sister, Alexis," I said, stepping to one side.

"How nice to meet you." Alexis extended her hand.

"What the hell's that?" Remy asked, pointing at Bubbles.

"You're going to be sorry you asked," I whispered.

"This is Bubbles. She's a Shorkie." Alexis held the dog out toward my neighbor.

"What the hell's a Shorkie?"

"Shorkies are designer dogs." My sister looked extremely pleased as she continued. "She's a cross between a Yorkshire Terrier and a Shi Tzu. Her parents were show champions."

"My wife's sister used to have a little dog," Remy said.

"Really? What..."

"Hated that damn dog. You ready to eat?" he said, looking at me. "Help yourself to a beer while I get the food on the table."

I led the way into the kitchen, grabbed two bottles

out of the fridge, and sat down at the table. "Are you just going to stand there holding that dog?"

"Uh, well..." Alexis looked around.

"Stick her in there." I pointed to her bag.

"But this isn't Bubbles' bag." She slid the huge purse off her shoulder and held it up.

"Come on, it's bigger than the one you had her in today. She'll be fine."

Alexis looked from the small dog in her left hand to the giant handbag in her right. "Here Precious," she said, stuffing Bubbles inside. "You climb in here while Mommy has dinner."

"Mommy?" Remy placed a platter of pork chops on the table and looked at me, his eyebrows raised. I shrugged and rolled my eyes. Shaking his head, he continued to carry food to the table. A big, yellow bowl of fluffy white potatoes was next, followed by a crock of steaming gravy. The last thing he added was a pyramid of corn-on-the-cob.

As Alexis surveyed the food before her, a horrified look came over her face. "I can't possibly eat any of..." She was interrupted by a loud growling sound — from her stomach. "Oh, excuse me. I must be hungrier than I thought."

"Just what a cook loves to hear," Remy said sitting down at the table.

"But I..." My sister again looked at the crunchy brown pork chops, mountain of mashed potatoes, and creamy gravy. "Do you have any salad?"

"Nope. Can't eat it so I don't make it. Dig in before it gets cold," Remy said, stabbing himself a chop off the pile of meat.

"Would you like to share an ear of corn?" Alexis asked me.

"Nope." I grabbed the top one off the pyramid and began slathering it with butter.

Using her thumb and forefinger, she gingerly picked up an ear and set it on her plate. Then she put a dab of potatoes next to it and drizzled a teaspoon of gravy over it.

"Here you go," Remy said, passing her the platter of pork chops. "Fried these up in bacon grease."

Alexis offered a weak smile and cut off a small piece of the one closest to her. "Do you have any Butterbuds?"

"Sure thing." He handed her a small plate with a cube of butter on it. "No, I need..." She looked over at me. I gave her a big smile and continued to gnaw on my ear of corn. "Never mind." She took a tiny taste of her potatoes and gravy. "Mmm, these are delicious."

"My wife's recipe. Used heavy whipping cream instead of milk. Makes them creamier."

"Heavy cream, huh?" She took another nibble. "They really are good." Then she picked up the small piece of pork. After contemplating it for at least a minute, she closed her mouth around the tiny morsel. "Oh, I haven't tasted anything like that for years."

"Well, then dig in; there's plenty. What you got there wouldn't satisfy that dog of yours." Then he plopped some potatoes on his own plate and drowned them in gravy.

A transformation slowly came over my sister. She helped herself to a good-sized pork chop and a heaping spoonful of potatoes, which she smothered with a generous serving of gravy. Then she took what had to be two tablespoons of butter and began painting her corn with it.

Remy chuckled as she proceeded to devour the food in front of her. "Sure do like to see a body enjoying a meal. Kinda reminds me of you the night we had stew."

Alexis looked at me and smiled. "Do you mind if I have one of those?" she asked, pointed to my beers.

I picked one up and handed it to her. "Are you sure you want this?" I said. "Do you know how many calories are in one of these?"

"Shut up." She grabbed the bottle, twisted off the top, and gulped it down.

"So how's your investigation of the jewel thief coming?" Remy asked.

"Oh, we solved that this afternoon. Or I should say, I did," Alexis said, wiping her mouth on the back of her hand.

"Really?" Remy's head rotated until he was looking me right in the eye.

I smiled. "Turns out Mary Littlefield, that's the resident who was taking the jewelry, and her son had been stealing from several convalescent hospitals over the past couple of years. The mother would take the pieces and then her son would pawn them. They never stayed in one place very long and that's why no one suspected them. It was purely by chance that we caught her with the jewelry."

"Thanks to my slippers," Alexis added.

"Uh-huh. And how about Gus?"

"Oh, we found his car and that poor dog," Alexis interjected between bites.

"You found Gus' car? How on earth did you manage that?"

"I took Raven cross-country to the head of Goose Creek. I planned to follow the creek down searching for clues, but instead I found his car and the cave where he'd been digging up the artifacts."

"What do you think happened?" Remy asked.

"There is evidence of a flash flood, and I'd be willing to bet that's what killed the dog. Looked like Gus had set up a makeshift camp, so I'm guessing he'd spent quite a lot of time there." I speared myself another pork chop. "As to what happened to him, I still don't know for sure. He took a blow to the head and had water in his lungs, but any evidence of someone else being there is long gone. The only thing I know for sure is that the mountain lion didn't get him."

"What mountain lion?" Alexis and Remy chorused.

"The one that had taken up residence in the cave. But don't worry," I said to Alexis, "it wasn't there today."

"Oh, that's comforting."

"What about the artifacts?" Remy asked.

"I still don't know why he was digging them up. I'm hoping to go back to the resort tomorrow and interview Tom Lowry."

"Resort?" Alexis asked. "What kind of resort?"

"It's more like a hotel. Fancy rooms with hot tubs."

"Maybe I should go along in case that Lowry guy isn't cooperative," Remy offered.

"Ooh, I'd love to see the resort." She clapped her hands together. "Maybe I can help solve this case too."

Remy glared at Alexis. "Look, I've been in on this one from the getgo. If anyone tags along, it should be me. What if there's trouble?"

"Trouble? From one guy? Besides," Alexis waved her ear of corn at me, "she carries a gun for goodness sake. What protection could an elderly gentleman like..."

"Elderly!" Remy slammed both hands on the table, and got to his feet. "Who the hell you calling elderly?"

"That's it!" I shoved my chair away from the table. "I'm going home."

"You can't leave her here," Remy called after me.

The hell I can't. I threw open the front door, stomped down the steps, and climbed into the Ford. Slamming it into first gear, I rumbled down the driveway, my jaw clenching and unclenching. As soon as I got home, I marched into the guest room. The sofa bed was open and covered with a lacy comforter that Alexis must have brought with her. Matching pillows were meticulously arranged on it. Looking around, I realized Alexis had re-arranged everything in the room. Everything, that is, except my Tae Kwon Do sparring dummy. Weighing at least a hundred pounds, it remained in the middle of the room where I'd put it.

After stripping down to my sports bra and briefs, I flipped the end of the mattress up and jammed the bed back into the sofa, scattering lacy pillows in all directions.

Twenty minutes later I was drenched in sweat and

my workout dummy had had a thorough beating. Feeling better, I donned my robe, grabbed a beer out of the fridge, and then headed to the bathhouse. Just before stepping into the sunken tub, I heard Alexis picking her way up the gravel driveway in her stiletto-heeled boots, babbling the whole time to that dust mop dog of hers. Quietly, I closed the door and slipped into the heated water.

Chapter 15

"Pop Tart or cereal bar?" I asked Alexis when she wandered into the kitchen the next morning, her pink-clad companion close behind.

"For what?"

"Breakfast. Which do you want?"

"Ugh, neither. Don't you have any wholegrain muffins? I'd even settle for a bagel and cream cheese."

That's a switch from the fat-craving monster I saw last night. "Sorry, been too busy to go shopping and there's no time to stop off at the Wagon Wheel."

"Well, I guess I'll try a cereal bar," Alexis said, pouring herself a cup of coffee.

I reached into the cupboard and pulled down a brightly colored box. "Looks like you'll have to settle for a Pop Tart. These are all gone," I said, turning the box upside down and shaking it.

"Fine, just give me something. I'm starving!" Alexis opened the silver packet I'd handed her and sniffed at its contents. "Are you going to the resort today? Can I come? I'd love to see it."

"I'm not so sure that's such a good idea. I don't know how long I'll be."

"Well, what if I follow you in my car and after I check out the resort, I'll drive into Cedarville. I saw the cutest little boutique on one of our trips through, and then I'll go grocery shopping and cook dinner."

"Since when do you cook?"

"Sarah, darling, I've been cooking gourmet meals for years."

"Gourmet, huh?"

"Don't worry. I'll make something you'll like. So, what do you say?"

"Fine, whatever. Just be ready to go by seven. I don't want to be waiting around for you."

"Not a problem. We'll be ready."

Oh, brother! "You can use the bathroom while I feed Raven. But don't be too long." I refilled my coffee cup, slipped on my rubber boots, and trudged down to the barn. As I approached the corral, Raven greeted me with his soft nicker. "And good morning to you big fella." I peeled off a flake of hay and threw it over the fence. Wanting to give my sister plenty of time to get out of my way, I leaned against the gate to sip my coffee and watch the black gelding chomp on his breakfast. "Be grateful you're out here," I told him. "You haven't had your life interrupted by visiting relatives."

The big horse swung his head up and chuckled at me.

"You're right, Raven. It is pretty funny." I dumped out the last of my coffee and headed back to the house.

Jumping into the shower, I let the hot water beat down on my head. The tension that had been building between my shoulder blades began to ease up. As I got dressed, I heard Alexis yapping at her dog. I could only imagine what she was doing to the poor mutt.

With no time to dry my hair, I pulled it back into a single braid and grabbed the last Pop Tart out of the box. Scarfing it down as I headed out the door, I was surprised, no make that shocked, to see my sister standing by her car, waiting for me.

"Here we are, ready to go. Aren't we Precious?" she asked her tortured pet. She'd dressed Bubbles in a green floral sundress trimmed with a purple ruffle and matching bow.

"What the — is that a tiara on her head?" I asked, as I got closer.

"Isn't it just adorable?"

"Yeah, adorable." I climbed into the Explorer and fired it up. Alexis hadn't even gotten her tiny dog into her tiny car before I pulled out of the driveway. But knowing how she drove, I knew she'd have no problem catching up, and I was right. I'd barely made it through Fort Bidwell when I heard a high-pitched "beep" behind me. *Even her horn is annoying.* I raised my hand and gave her a quick wave of acknowledgement. Then I set the cruise control at fifty and waited.

Sibling rivalry never does die and it rarely grows up. I knew my speed-demon sister would go nuts at such a slow rate. I also knew she couldn't go screaming around me because she didn't know where we were going. My mean streak was showing and I was enjoying it.

Looking in the rearview mirror, I saw her talking non-stop and assumed it was directed at the dog rather than herself or me. As we traveled south, she drummed her fingers on the steering wheel. Then she leaned her elbow on the door and rested her chin in her left hand. Finally she threw her hands in the air and started talking again.

Taking this as my cue, I stomped on the accelerator and kicked it up to almost seventy. Alexis stuck right with me, a big smile on her face. Unfortunately, her pleasure was short-lived; we pulled into the resort a couple of minutes later.

"Gosh Granny, could you drive any slower?" she said, climbing out of her car. "Is this it? This is a resort? Are you kidding me?"

"Don't be too quick to judge. Wait until you check out the inside."

"Well I hope the inside is more impressive than... do you smell that?"

"What?"

"Coffee. I smell coffee, and not that insipid Folgers,

either." Alexis took a deep breath. "This is..." She inhaled again. "What I smell is a robust, bold coffee. I've got to find out where that smell is coming from." She scooped Bubbles into her arms and started for the front door.

I hurried after her, hoping to reach the building before she did, but she'd traded her precarious footwear for flat-soled shoes and moved much faster than usual. Still, I managed to overtake her. Passing through the entryway, I left my sister to experience the unique arrangement of foliage and furniture. "Good morning," I said when I spotted the petite proprietor.

Abigail Flowers looked up from the table she was setting. "Oh, it's you. Good morning, deputy. I'll bet you've come back to talk to Tom." She laid the handful of silverware on the table and joined me at the check-in desk.

"Yes, ma'am."

"Well, he's... oh, what an adorable dog."

I turned to find my sister standing behind me, a huge grin on her face. "Isn't she, though."

"I'd love to get a little dog like this, but Ed would just pitch a fit. He says they're nothing but a nuisance."

Smart guy, that Ed.

"What kind of dog is she?" Mrs. Flowers asked.

"She's a designer dog — a Shorkie."

I felt a familiar twinge of pain behind my left eye.

"Oh, I've heard of those. A cross between a Shi Tzu and Yorkshire Terrier."

"Why, yes. You do know your designer dogs."

"And what a pretty outfit. Wherever do you find such adorable clothes?"

My neck began to tense.

"Well, there's a specialty shop in San Francisco that carries some things, but my mother buys most of Bubbles' clothes."

"Mom?" I interrupted. "Mom is the one who buys that stuff for your dog?"

"Of course. She says that until you give her

grandchildren she might as well spoil Bubbles." Alexis smiled at the small dog and bounced her up and down like a baby.

"Me, give her grandchildren? What about you?"

"Oh, Mother knows how important my career is right now."

"Your career? What about — never mind. Abigail, you were saying where I might find..."

"Are you the one brewing that wonderfully smelling coffee?" Alexis asked.

"Why, yes. We just installed our new espresso machine a couple of days ago, and I was trying it out."

"Espresso? Did you say espresso?" Alexis' eyes glazed over like a kid in a candy store.

"I sure did. I'm trying this new blend I found on our last trip to the valley. It's called Casi Cielo."

"Are you kidding me? That's my favorite, so rich and full-bodied."

"I thought so, too. Would you like to try some?"

The tension spread out toward my shoulder blades. *Unbelievable.* "Uh, Mrs. Flowers," I began. When I didn't get a response, I tried a more direct approach. "Abigail, where will I find Tom?"

"Oh my, I'm so sorry. I completely forgot all about you, dear. You'll find him around back in the service alley between the units. Here — excuse me just a moment, dear," she said to Alexis.

"Not a problem, Abigail. Go right ahead. We'll wait right here for you."

She walked me through the entryway. "Go out the front door, turn to the right and follow the narrow walkway to the back of the building. You'll see a fence between the two wings of rooms. The gate should be open and you'll find him inside."

"Thank you. Don't be a pest, Alexis," I called as I opened the door.

"Me a pest? Are you kidding me?"

Certain I'd heard that somewhere before, I followed

Abigail's instructions and located the opened gate. Stepping inside, I also located Tom Lowry.

The man was a couple inches short of six feet and had straight black hair, which he wore pulled back in a ponytail. He was dressed in faded Levis, an old chambray work shirt, and a pair of moccasins that looked like they'd traveled from one end of Surprise Valley to the other. A small leather pouch hung from a strip of rawhide tied around his neck.

"Excuse me, sir. Are you Tom Lowry?"

"Who wants to know?" the man asked without looking up. As he swept out the private patio, the muscles of his forearms flexed under his bronze skin.

"I'm Deputy Murdock and I'm investigating the death of Gus Miller."

"I heard he'd gotten himself killed." He leaned the broom against the cedar fence, and stepped out into the service alley. His beak-like nose bent at least two different directions between the bridge and the tip, and a deep scar ran down the left side of his face, connecting his eye to his upper lip. "What happened to him?"

"That's why I'm here. I'm trying to locate anyone who may have known him."

"Well, hell everyone knew old Gus. What good's that gonna do you?" He stood facing me with his arms folded across his chest, as if daring me to answer.

"Right now I'm attempting to come up with some kind of timeline of his activities before he was killed. Did you know Gus every well?"

"We tipped a few together, mostly over at the Silver Spur."

"When was the last time you saw him?"

"Hell, lady I don't remember." He left the service alley and headed toward a row of small rabbit hutches, but I wasn't giving up that easily.

"Did you see him around Christmas?" I asked, following along behind him.

"Christmas? Neither one of us ever had much to do

with Christmas." He spun the knob of a nearby spigot and began filling water dishes with a hose.

"How about New Year's?"

The slightest hint of a smile crossed his face. "Yeah, I believe we tied on a good one that night." Having reached the end of the row, he dropped the hose and turned off the water.

"Was that before or after your argument with him?"

Tom narrowed his eyes but didn't reply. Instead he opened one of the cages and removed a small brown rabbit. It curled up in a ball and tucked its nose into the crook of his arm.

"Was Gus a collector of Native American artifacts?"

"How's that?" he asked, stroking the tiny creature's back.

"I found several boxes of artifacts when I searched his house and I was wondering..."

"You searched his house?" His hand stopped mid-stroke.

"That's right. I was looking for anything that might tell me what he'd been doing prior to his death."

"So what'd you do with the stuff you found?"

"Don't worry. I confiscated it and as soon as my investigation is concluded, it'll be turned over to the proper authorities."

"Uh huh." The man locked the rabbit back in its cage and began to turn away.

"Just one more thing and I'll let you get back to work," I said, opening the folder I'd brought with me. "Have you by chance seen any of these people?" I handed him the pictures Sue had sent me. As he flipped through them, I thought I noticed a flicker of recognition, but it lasted no more than a second.

"Sorry, don't know any of them," he said, thrusting the pictures at me. He began running the fingers of his left hand along his scar. "Now if you don't mind, I have things to do." He re-entered the private patio and began sweeping again.

"Certainly. Thank you, Mr. Lowry." I left the service alley and started back toward the front door. I rounded the corner just in time to see Alexis drive off, throwing gravel everywhere. Glad to be on my own again, I entered the building.

Walking into the small lobby of the resort, I had to admit the coffee did smell delicious, but I had work to do. I found Abigail putting out the last of the silverware.

"Mrs. Flowers," I began, crossing the large room. "I hope my sister didn't take up too much of your time."

"Oh not at all, dear. We had a lovely visit, and she gave me all kinds of ideas for our new dining room."

"I'm glad she was helpful. If you have a moment, ma'am, I'd like to show you some pictures and see whether or not you recognize any of them."

"Certainly, let me just grab my glasses. They're right over here."

I followed her to the small check-in desk and watched her rummage around under the counter. As she perched her reading glasses on the end of her nose, I pulled out the pictures I'd shown to Tom. "Have you seen any of these people before?" I asked, handing her the stack.

"Oh, my. These aren't the friendliest faces I've ever seen. Who are these — wait a moment, I believe I know this man." She handed one of the pictures back to me and continued through the rest of the stack. "Hmm, I think I know this one too, but there's something that's not quite right. I know, he had a mustache when I saw him."

As I took the other picture from her, it was difficult to keep my composure; I might actually have a lead. "Mrs. Flowers, where did you see these men?"

"Why right here. They were guests."

"How long ago?"

"Oh, dear. I'm not sure. I know it was before the holidays because the kitchen wasn't finished yet. You know, those men weren't very nice about that either."

"I'm sure they weren't. Do you happen to remember why they came to Surprise Valley?"

"I'm sorry, I sure don't. They didn't mention it when they checked in, and they tended to keep to themselves." Abigail removed her glasses and stashed them back under the counter. "You know, Tom may be able to help you. He seemed to hit it off with them. I saw them speaking to him several times."

"I see. Well, thanks again for your help." I turned and started for the door then stopped. "If you see either of these men again, would you mind giving me a call?" I asked, pulling out one of my cards and handing it to her. "I'd really appreciate it."

"Not at all, dear. I'll be happy to help, but I'm not sure they'll come back."

"I understand. Just in case, huh?"

"Of course, my dear. Of course."

Chapter 16

Driving north on County Road 1, I couldn't help thinking I'd missed something at Gus' place. I had no idea what it could be, but I felt like I needed to take another look around. My woman's intuition, as Hensley would call it — or worse.

I turned left onto the road to Lake City and pulled up in front of the dilapidated house. The crime tape was still in place as well as the locks.

Rummaging in the back of the Explorer, I found a small pry bar. After rolling up my sleeves, I began pulling the sheets of plywood off the windows. I wanted as much light in that place as I could get.

Thirty minutes later, I had a pile of splintered plywood, three bruised and bleeding knuckles, and a sweaty brow. I unlocked both doors and opened them as far as they would go, providing a way out for as many rodents as possible.

The kitchen looked about the same as it did when Remy and I first poked around. Fortunately, the added light from the windows seemed to keep the furry creatures at bay. I looked through all the cupboards, using the pry bar to move things aside, finding nothing but rat feces and rotting food.

Moving into the dining area, I was surprised at how much bigger the house seemed in the bright daylight. An old chandelier, covered with lacy cobwebs, hung over the table. The couch and chair on the other side of the room looked even more disgusting than before. Each was covered with stains of unknown origin, and the upholstery had tufts of stuffing popping out all over.

The stairway, with most of its balusters missing, looked treacherous. As I got to the top, I glanced toward the spare room. The door was standing open, just like we had left it, but something else made my heart skip a beat. There, in the thick dust that had accumulated on the floor, was a set of unusual prints made by a shoe with a pointed toe and square heel. If it weren't for the large size, I'd have sworn the print had been left by a pair of my sister's fashion boots.

Instinctively, I reached down and unfasten the strap on my 9 mm. With my right hand resting on the butt of my gun, I slowly approached the room. As I got closer, I could tell that there were two sets of prints — one in each direction. Whoever had gone into the room had come back out. *But how did they get in here?* I had undone the locks myself; there had been no sign of forced entry.

Standing to one side, so as to not disturb any evidence, I peered into the room. Nothing appeared to have been moved. The trail of dusty prints wound around the piles of furniture toward the end of the room. That's when I noticed that two panes of the window had been broken out as well as the wooden trim that had held it them in place. I could see that the dust on the large trunk just in front of the window had also been disturbed. Someone had been in the house!

Moving quickly, I entered Gus' bedroom. Expecting to see it ransacked, I was surprised to find everything just as it had been on my previous visit.

Then I remembered the bathroom. The mere thought of the repulsive little room made me gag, but it was the only area left to check.

At the bottom of the stairs I took a closer look at the nearly invisible tracks of Remy's smooth-soled work boots and my own Vibram-soled shoes. Here and there I could barely make out a partial print like the ones upstairs.

As soon as the bathroom door was opened however, it was obvious someone had been in there. A tall stack of newspapers had been knocked over, scattering the periodicals everywhere. With them out of the way, I could see a small door had been cut into the wall, and judging from its location, I guessed it allowed access into the area under the stairs.

Pulling the Maglite off my belt, I crouched down and peered inside. At least two different shoe patterns were visible on the filthy floor. The number and direction of the prints indicated that several trips had been made into the hidden room, but the most recent ones were a match to those I'd seen upstairs.

As I moved the beam of light, the skittering of small feet made the hairs on the back of my neck stand at attention. Torn between my disgust for rodents and the need to look for clues, I hesitated, took a deep breath, and eased further into the cramped space. As I straightened up, cobwebs brushed my face and stuck in my hair.

The prints branched off into three separate trails, each one ending at a rectangular-shaped outline pressed into the dust. Scanning the floor, I found a small piece of obsidian stuck between the floorboards. Whatever had been hidden in there was long gone. The question of the day was who had taken it and why. Careful not to disturb anything, I ducked through the small door and went out to my rig to retrieve the digital camera.

The sun was directly overhead and the warmth beating down on my shoulders felt good. It felt so good, I hated to go back inside, but I needed photos of the shoe prints for comparison later.

Gazing off into the distance I became aware of a small pickup parked about a quarter of a mile down the road. I reached back into the Explorer for my binoculars. When I looked through them, I was surprised to find the driver watching me through a pair of his own. In a split second, he started his rig and sped off in a cloud of dust. I didn't recognize the vehicle but figured its ugly burnt orange color and primered back fender would make it easy to identify, if and when I ever saw it again.

Before going back inside, I walked around the weatherworn house, hoping to discover how the mystery visitor had gained access. Under the second-story window, I found a ladder that had to be as old as the building itself. The two-by-fours it had been built from were gray and splitting. The fact that it hadn't fallen apart when it was used told me whoever climbed on it couldn't have been very heavy. Examining the rungs more closely, I saw some kind of substance stuck to some of them. I returned to the Explorer and grabbed my evidence case. After taking some photos, and gathering a couple of samples, I went back inside.

A few minutes later I'd re-secured Gus's house, stowed my equipment, and was heading for Cedarville and the Wagon Wheel Café. With my Pop Tart only a memory, a burger with all the trimmings and a side of home fries was sounding real good.

I'd almost finished my lunch when Remy walked in. He stepped over to the counter, his eyes darting from one end of the place to the other.

"You here alone?" he whispered as he got settled in the low-backed chair next to me.

"Why do you ask?" I knew the answer but didn't see any harm giving him a hard time.

"'Cause if your sister is here, I ain't gonna be, that's why."

"Sit back and relax. She's supposed to be shopping for some gourmet meal she's cooking tonight. Want to come to dinner?"

"Not on your life. And I'm afraid you won't be getting an invite until after she's long gone."

"I understand, believe me."

Sal appeared and set a glass of water in front of Remy. "What'll it be?"

"What's the special today?"

"Cookie's got a nice mess of liver and onions going."

I grimaced.

"Dish me up some — and throw on some fried taters."

Remy picked up his water glass and drained it. "You go back to the resort today and talk to Tom?"

"Sure did and I went back to Gus' place too."

"What in the hell would you want to go back to that rat-infested place for?"

"I just wanted to take another look around, see if we'd missed anything." I popped the last french fry into my mouth. "I even pulled off those sheets of plywood to get a better look."

"Now, see there. You needed my help."

I covered my bruised knuckles with my other hand. "I managed. I will say the place sure looked different in full sunlight."

"How's that?"

"Scarier, and a lot more disgusting."

"Mmm, find that hard to believe." Remy's lunch arrived and he squirted a large dollop of yellow mustard onto his plate.

Checking my watch, I figured I had plenty of time to make a trip to Alturas before Alexis' gourmet meal. "Well, Remy I've got to go to the office and speak with the sheriff."

"You let me know when that sister of yours leaves and I'll make you the best dang dinner you've ever had."

"It's a deal. Thanks." I paid my tab, got settled into the Explorer, and headed up the mountain. The winding road helped me fight the feeling of drowsiness brought on by the warm sun and my full stomach. By the time I reached the office, I knew exactly how I was going to present my case.

Grabbing the evidence I'd collected and the digital camera, I went inside. "Hey, Josh," I said as I entered the lab. "Any chance you can process this stuff and print out some digital photos I've got on my memory card?"

"Sure thing. You caught me at a good time, nothing in the hopper."

"Great. I have to go see Sheriff Atkins, and then I'll stop by and pick up what you've got." I opened my evidence case and handed over my camera and a small vial.

"Now there may be a problem."

"What's that?"

"Sheriff Atkins got called to Redding. He's not due back for a couple of days."

"Who's the watch commander?"

"Undersheriff Sandusky. His office is two doors down from Atkins' next to the head."

"Gotcha. Thanks." I hadn't run into the undersheriff since he outfitted me with the old equipment. Between the two cases I'd been working on, our paths hadn't crossed, so I didn't know much about him. When I saw Scott sitting in the break room, I took the opportunity to learn what I could.

"Hey, Deputy Jenkins," I said. "Made any trips to Redding lately?"

"Very funny, Sarah. You're quite a comedienne."

"I knew you'd appreciate my sense of humor." I stepped closer and lowered my voice. "Actually I was hoping you could fill me in on someone."

"Well, I've been on the force for a while now. Who do you want to know about?" He'd gotten a package of pink snowballs out of the vending machine and was in the process of engorging one.

"Sandusky."

Scott coughed twice, gulped once, and began choking on his mouthful of pink and brown goo. Just as I was about to give him the Heimlich, he managed to clear his throat.

"Gee whiz, you practically killed me." He stepped over to the sink, stuck his head under the tap, and took several swallows of water. "What do you want to know about Dirk the Jerk for?" he whispered, drying his mouth on his sleeve and leaving streaks of pink marshmallow behind.

"The Miller case, you know, the DB you drove to

Redding, may have just gotten more complicated. I think the guy was involved with a group that sells illegally acquired Indian artifacts. If so, the whole thing needs to be turned over to the FBI."

"You really should wait for Sheriff Atkins to get back. Trust me, you don't ever want to mention the FBI to Sandusky. I mean you should have heard him rant and rave when he found out you were..." He broke off his sentence and gave me that damn crooked smile of his.

"Because I'm a woman?"

"Well, that's only part of it. He's always mouthing off about no female's ever going to back him up if he can help it. But that's not the only reason. He applied to the bureau about ten years ago but didn't get accepted. Something about not being able to pass the psychological evaluation."

At that moment everything fell into place and I knew I was going to be at a disadvantage even before I started. "We need to contact the proper authorities right away. It will take several days before someone from the Art Crime Team can be mobilized, and that's only if they feel it's necessary."

"Hey I understand all that, but if I were in your shoes I'd wait. Sandusky can be very unreasonable at times, especially when he's in charge. Some of us even call him the 'Frank Burns' of Modoc County."

"I'll take your advice into consideration, Scott. And thanks for the heads up."

"You bet," he said, picking up the other pink snowball. I left him to enjoy the rest of his snack and went in search of the undersheriff.

Dirk Sandusky wasn't the ugliest man I'd ever seen, but he'd be hard-pressed to buy lunch with his looks. A tall man, his slight build did not make him formidable, and his close-set eyes gave him a quizzical look. The only aspect of his appearance that emitted authority was his military-style haircut.

Standing before the closed door of his office, I

hesitated. Maybe Scott was right. Maybe I should wait for the sheriff to get back. But what about the evidence? How could Sandusky argue with that? Determined I had enough to convince the man, I rapped on the door. When there was no answer, I rapped again — this time a little harder.

"Enter."

I opened the door and stepped inside. "Undersheriff Sandusky?"

At the sound of my voice, his head sprang up and his face deepened in color. "Murdock! What are you doing here? Why aren't you out on patrol?"

"Well, sir," I began, moving further into the room. "I needed to speak with Sheriff Atkins about my current investigation."

"He's not here right now."

"Yes sir, I know. That's why I came to see you. I think you need to contact the — that is I think..."

"Spit it out, Murdock. I don't have all day!" He closed the file he'd been reading and put down his pen.

"I believe that Gus Miller was acquiring Indian artifacts to be sold illegally."

"And you know this because..."

"The owner of the High Desert Hot Springs identified two known dealers of stolen Indian artifacts."

"And just how was this person able to make this identification?" He stroked his short, bristly mustache.

This is going to be harder than I thought. "I obtained photos of known suspects linked to illegal trafficking of stolen artifacts and..."

"Cut to the chase, Murdock. Where did you get the photos?"

"An acquaintance who's with the FBI."

"Is that following proper procedure, Deputy, or were you using woman's intuition to guide you?" His lips curled into a sneer, reminding me of Richard Hensley. "Did the sheriff authorize that?"

"Well, no sir. It was just a hunch I was pursuing.

Anyway, Mrs. Flowers identified two of the people as former guests of her establishment." I knew this was my only chance, so I took a deep breath and continued. "She also reported that they were seen speaking with Tom Lowry, a known associate of Gus Miller. Several boxes of Indian artifacts were recovered from Gus' house, so you see it is highly probable that this case involves the illegal selling of those artifacts and the FBI should be notified immediately."

"Whoa, whoa there." Sandusky held up both hands. "Don't get your pantyhose in a knot. You said it is probable that the case is tied to these alleged artifact dealers. Do you have any proof?"

"Not yet, but if these men return..."

"Look, Murdock let's not make a federal case out of this." He picked up his pen and reopened the file that was sitting in front of him. "When Sheriff Atkins returns, I'll bring your concerns to his attention."

"But Title 18 of the FBI legislation clearly states..."

Sandusky sprang from his chair with such force he sent it crashing into the oak bookcase behind him. "Do not stand there and quote FBI regulations to me," he yelled, leaning far enough across his desk I could tell he'd had onions for lunch. "Dismissed!"

I'd gone too far. As I spun on my heel, I could feel the heat rising from my chest to my forehead. Instead of heading back to the lab, I turned to the right and marched into the ladies' room. Clearing the door, I gave the white metal garbage can a savage kick. It hurled across the tile floor and slammed into the wall on the far side of the room, scattering paper towels in all directions. I was sure Sandusky heard the loud clattering as it reverberated in the small sanctuary, but I didn't care.

I leaned back against the cool wall, crossed my arms over my chest and closed my eyes. Taking deep controlled breaths, I was able to slow my heart rate and get my anger under control. A few moments later, I returned to the lab to see what Josh had for me.

"Just in time, Deputy," he said as I entered the room. "Your pictures are almost done and I've identified the substance you collected. It's commonly found on cattle ranches as well as most drinking establishments on a Friday night."

I frowned at him. "Sorry?"

"You know, bullshit."

"Oh yeah, right." *Scott's warped sense of humor must be rubbing off on this kid.*

"Whoever made these prints," he continued, picking up the photos from my camera, "has worn these boots for a long time. See the odd shape of the heel? That's due to excessive wear. And the round pattern here? I'd be willing to bet the guy's sock is touching the ground every time he takes a step. Definitely time for a new pair of cowboy boots."

"Cowboy boots? These were made by cowboy boots?"

"Yep. Nothing fancy either. Probably Justins or maybe an old pair of Ropers."

"Well, thanks Josh," I said as I gathered up what I considered useless information. I was looking for someone who wore old cowboy boots and walked around in bovine excrement. That fit just about every resident in Surprise Valley.

Chapter 17

When I opened my front door, I was greeted by complete silence. Alexis and Bubbles were nowhere in sight, but I knew they had come back because the Z3 was in the driveway and the living room was littered with tissue, boxes, and bags from the boutique she wanted to check out. Every piece of furniture had at least three coordinated outfits carefully arranged on it.

Hoping they'd gone for a walk, I traded my uniform for an oversized T-shirt and a pair of cutoff sweats and went to grab a beer out of the fridge.

Good to her word, Alexis had indeed gone grocery shopping and my refrigerator was stuffed with all kinds of food. Unfortunately, she'd shoved all the beer to the back and I had to empty most of the top shelf to find it.

A promising beginning, the day had quickly gone into the crapper, and I needed a long soak. Sliding my feet into a pair of flip-flops, I headed for the bathhouse. Just as I reached my tiny sanctuary, I realized it was occupied. Opening the door, I was shocked to see not only Alexis in my custom-built hot tub, but her dog as well. The petite pooch was dressed in a miniature version of its owner's black and white zebra-stripe bikini.

"What the hell are you doing?" I demanded.

"I thought a dip in this deliciously warm water would feel terrific after a day of power shopping. Would you like to join us?"

"No I would not. Get out of my tub and take that with

you," I said, pointing to Bubbles as she made another lap around her makeshift pool.

"There's plenty of room for all of us. Why are you being so mean?"

"I'm not being mean. I've had a bitch of a day, and I just need some time to myself. Besides, aren't you suppose to be cooking dinner?"

"What time is it?"

"It's after five." I grabbed Alexis' towel and held it out for her.

"Wow, where did the time go? No wonder I'm all pruny," she said holding her hands up for inspection. Plucking Bubbles out of the water as she swam by, my sister climbed out of the hot tub, pulled the towel around her and the dog, and hustled toward the house.

Before stepping into the warm water, I set my beer on the edge and wondered if Bubbles' potty training included pools. Hoping for the best, I submerged myself and stretched out. As I floated weightlessly, I went over the events of the day. Was Gus digging up artifacts for the men Abigail had identified? How was Tom involved, and why did he lie? And who broke into Gus' house and what did he take? Then there was the matter of the Undersheriff. My gut instinct told me Gus was involved in a much larger operation and the FBI should be notified. A quick email to Sue at the bureau was all it would take to get someone to come to Surprise Valley. What I wasn't so sure about was whether or not the sheriff would see it that way, or would he side with the undersheriff?

I finished off my beer and allowed myself to sink to the bottom of the hot tub. I'd left the bureau to avoid getting into just such a situation again. Moving here, I'd hoped to do my job and spend the rest of my time riding my horse. The plan had been so simple. So much for simple.

A familiar rumbling deep in my stomach told me it was time to check on Alexis and her gourmet meal. I climbed out, pulled my clothes back on, and headed for the house. As soon as I opened the door, I knew something was wrong. A foul odor permeated the small dwelling, and the clanging of pans and incessant chatter warned me Alexis had probably bitten off more than she could chew. *No pun intended.*

Peering into the kitchen, I saw that my assumptions were correct. My sister was bouncing between the counter, stove, and refrigerator like an out-of-control pinball, while her dog ran in circles, dodging her feet. Since it was obvious that dinner wasn't quite ready, I decided to take advantage of the delay and sit down at my computer.

I thought about retrieving another beer from the fridge, but the smell of something burning was a clear indicator that the kitchen was not the best place to be at the moment. Checking my email, I was surprised to find a message from Sue. Apparently an increase in activity by some of the men she'd told me about had people at the bureau anticipating some kind of big score. She also asked if I'd had any luck with the pictures she sent me. Such a perfect opportunity! I could let Sue know what I'd found out without initiating the correspondence. I clicked on the reply button and briefly shared with her the information the owner of the resort had given me. Not wanting a confrontation, I recommended she contact Sheriff Atkins to advise him of the bureau's concerns. Satisfied that I'd done what I could, I shut down my computer and ventured into the kitchen.

What a mess! Splatters of food covered the floor, counters, and stove, and a thin layer of smoke hovered just below the ceiling. Every pan I owned had been used and then tossed into the sink, forming an unsteady pyramid of stainless steel. And Alexis was nowhere in sight.

Making the most of the situation, I tiptoed across the kitchen, opened the fridge, and freed another beer from the top shelf. After taking a long draw, I again smelled a most unpleasant odor. Glancing at the stove, I figured it was something Alexis had spilled on one of the burners.

As I sat down at the table, my sister swept into the room. Her face was still quite red, but her hair was freshly combed and she'd put on one of the outfits I'd seen in the other room. "Oh good, you're done. Just sit right there and help yourself to the wine." She pointed to an opened bottle. "I'll get the food on the table."

"Okay. What is for dinner, anyway?"

"You'll see." She grabbed two plates from the refrigerator and set them on the table. Each one had a pile of pink and green kale.

"Can you eat this stuff?" I asked, poking at the salad with my fork. "Isn't this what restaurants use as decoration on their buffets?"

"Wait until you taste this. You're in for quite a treat."

I continued to poke around in the pastel-colored leaves while Alexis pulled the rest of dinner out of the oven. One pot had large clumps of pasta, but it was so cemented together I couldn't tell what kind it was. Next came a lumpy white sauce that resembled some cottage cheese I'd mistakenly opened two months after its pull date.

"I had a little trouble regulating the burners on your stove," she said, as she set a plate of broccoli on the table. Leaning closer, I saw that it had been badly scorched.

"You start on your salad, and I'll dish your plate," Alexis said.

"Uh — okay." Thrusting my fork into the kale, it took three tries, each one with a little more force, before I was able to pierce the colorful leaves. Slowly I closed my mouth around the bite and began to chew. Sand instantly filled every crevice of my mouth. I leaped to my feet and spat the gritty mess into the sink.

"What the hell is that?" I asked.

"Don't you like it?" Alexis' eyes filled with tears.

"It's full of sand. Didn't you wash it?"

"Of course I did. I mean I think I did. I was having

such a hard time with the stove. Forget the salad. Come try the Alfredo."

I walked back over to the table and sat down. The sight and smell of the stuff on my plate made my stomach turn. "Alexis, I can't eat this."

"I'm sure it tastes better than it looks."

"Have you tried it?"

"Well, no — not yet."

"Then how do you know how it tastes? I'll bet your dog wouldn't even eat this."

"Oh, you are so mean! I don't know why I try to do anything nice for you." Alexis grabbed the bottle of wine, stomped to her room, and slammed the door. Bubbles, who had been lying next to her food dish, raised her head.

"Can you believe that?" I asked the small dog. "If anyone should cry over this meal, it's me." I grabbed two more beers out of the fridge and positioned myself on the sofa in front of the television. As I mindlessly surfed the channels, the smell of lavender wafted into the room. Hitting the mute button on the remote, the sound of crashing waves bounced against the walls. I could just picture my sister supine on the foldout bed, her pink satin sleep mask on her face.

Bubbles wandered through the living room on her way to the room she shared with her owner. The sound of a rather large wave crashing on the shore made the mutt stop. She looked toward the closed door and then back at me. Spinning around, she jumped onto the sofa and plopped down next to me. "Good choice," I said. "I would've done the same thing."

So dark — can't see. Where's the phone? I hear it ringing. I'm lying down but when I open my eyes, I'm looking at myself lying in a hospital bed. What's happened, and why is the phone still ringing?

There's a man in a white coat next to the bed, but I can't see what he's doing. I drift to the left. He's leaning over the oxygen tank. Why won't he answer the phone? I see him turn a knob. Suddenly there's pressure on my chest — I can't catch my breath. I reach for the phone, but I can't move my arm. Who is that man? What is he doing? Stop it, I can't breathe. Answer the phone. Slowly he raises his head. It's — it's Hensley! And he's trying to kill me. Help!

Jerked out of the temporary coma of sleep, I realized the phone was really ringing, but I couldn't sit up. Bubbles had stretched out across my chest. Finally, I managed to shake her off and went in search of the phone. When I didn't find it perched in the charger, I followed the sound into the kitchen where I found it hiding under a discarded hand towel. Hoping it wasn't an emergency, I hit the talk button. "Hello?"

"Hello cupcake. I got your message." The man was practically purring.

"Who is this?" I demanded.

"Come on, sugarplum. You know who this is."

"Identify yourself, now."

"Alexis?" The purr turned into a whine.

"No, this is her sister."

"Oops, sorry. Is she there?"

"Who are you?"

"My name is Sterling Broderick. I'm her..."

"Boyfriend. Yeah, she told me all about you."

"All good, I hope."

Good grief. "Hang on, I'll get her for you." I made my way to the spare bedroom and opened the door. Alexis, still in her clothes, was lying spread-eagle on top of her lacy comforter sound asleep.

"Alexis," I said, shaking her gently. "Alexis, wake up. You have a phone call." When my sister didn't move, I shook her harder. "Alexis, get up. Sterling is on the phone."

She sat straight up as if an alarm clock had gone off. "Sterling? Now?"

"Here!" I thrust the phone at her and went to bed.

The next morning my head felt fuzzy, and the bright light hurt my eyes. Squinting at the clock, I saw I had overslept and was now two hours late for work.

I jumped into the shower and got dressed as quickly as I could. Poking my head into the spare room, I was surprised to find it void of all my sister's paraphernalia. "Alexis?" I called as I hurried out to the kitchen. It was still a wreck, littered with the remnants of last night's disaster. The only clean area on the counter was the spot where Alexis had put the dog food container. It was gone as well as Bubbles' dishes. My sister had packed up and left in the middle of the night without saying goodbye. That I could live with but not the mess she'd left behind. I hated to leave it until evening, but I had no choice. I was late for work.

Chapter 18

"What the hell happened to you?" Remy asked as I joined him at the counter of the Wagon Wheel Café.

"That bad, huh?" I said, plucking a menu out of the rack. "Rough night and the morning hasn't gone much better. My house is trashed, my sister skipped out on me, I haven't eaten since lunchtime yesterday, and I was late for work this morning."

"Did you say your sister's gone?"

"Yes I did. Left while I was sleeping."

"Yippee!!"

"Remy!"

"Well, I'm sorry, but..."

"Relax," I chuckled. "I feel the same way. It's just..."

"What can I get for you, deputy?" Sal stood before me, her pen poised over her pad.

"Give me a club sandwich, order of fries and a side of potato salad."

"Something to drink?"

"Diet Pepsi."

"Coming right up."

"It's just what?" Remy prodded.

"Huh? Oh, she shows up uninvited, turns my life upside down and my kitchen into a war zone and is gone in the blink of an eye."

"Well, I say good riddance to bad rubbish. Any luck on Gus' case?"

"Not really. I might have a lead, but it may turn out to be nothing."

"Here you are, deputy," Sal said, plopping my lunch down in front of me. Each quarter of my sandwich had to be four inches across. It, along with the double scoop of potato salad, was buried under a mountain of golden brown fries that made my mouth water. I was just about to sink my teeth into the toasted bread when my cell phone rang. I sighed, set down my sandwich, and answered it. "Murdock."

"Deputy, it's Abigail Flowers."

"Hello, Mrs. Flowers. What can I do for you?" I popped a french fry in my mouth.

"They're back."

"I'm sorry, ma'am. Who's back?" I forked in a bite of salad next.

"Those men. You know, in the pictures."

Nearly choking, I cleared my throat. "They're there right now?"

"Yes. I didn't recognize the name on the reservation, but I'm certain it's them."

"Where are they?"

"In their room. They checked in a few minutes ago. Are we in any kind of danger?" Her voice quavered ever so slightly.

"No ma'am. I don't believe so. Go on about your business and I'll be right there."

"But won't that spook them off? Don't you want to stake them out and see what they're up to?" Abigail asked.

I lowered my cell phone and turned to Remy. "You don't have a sister, do you?"

He frowned and shook his head.

"Huh." I put the phone back to my ear. "Mrs. Flowers, I'll be there in a few minutes and do some surveillance. What vehicle are they driving?"

"They flew into the airport, so they're using of one

of our resort vehicles — a brown Dodge Aries K. Do you want the license number?"

"No, ma'am. That won't be necessary." I recalled that all the resort vehicles had door-panel signs advertising the place. "Thanks for calling."

"Certainly, dear. Good-bye." I snapped my cell phone shut and put it away. "Sal," I called down the counter, "I need a take-out box." Then I worked on devouring my potato salad while I waited.

"Well?" Remy asked.

"Well what?" I said around a mouthful of food.

"What was that all about?"

"While I was at the resort, I asked the owner to look at some photos I'd gotten from a friend at the FBI, and she recognized two of them. These men are suspected of dealing in stolen artifacts, and she thinks they just checked in."

"No kidding. So are you going over there to check it out?"

I laughed. "She suggested I should put the place under surveillance."

"I like the way she thinks."

"I thought you might.

"So what are you going to do?"

"I'll probably drive over there and hang out for a while. See if those really are the men I'm looking for and what they're up to."

"You're not exactly dressed for undercover work, and won't they get suspicious with a sheriff's unit parked nearby?"

"I suppose I could park a distance away and watch through my binoculars."

"What if you could get closer without attracting attention?"

"And how would I do that?"

"Let me drive you over there in my rig. That way no one will pay us no mind and you can eat your lunch on the way."

I looked down at my plate of food, and my stomach growled. It was probably a false alarm anyway, and I was still hungry. "Remy what would I do without you?" I scooted my sandwich and fries into the box and threw Sal a ten-dollar bill. Then Remy and I piled into his Land Cruiser and headed for the resort. By the time we got there, I'd eaten most of my fries and all but one quarter of my sandwich. Stuffed, I closed the lid on the Styrofoam box and stashed it under my seat.

Remy pulled through the parking lot and backed into a spot on the far side of the row of parked cars. We had a perfect view of the front door as well as the brown sedan. Suffering from my lack of sleep, I slumped down in my seat and closed my eyes.

"Is that how they teach you to keep an eye on someone at the FBI?" Remy asked.

"Give me a break. Besides, I don't need to watch. I've got you."

"Glad you see it that way. Saves me time trying to convince you."

"Very funny. Just let me know if something happens."

"Well, consider yourself notified."

Sitting up, I saw two men walking away from the resort. Both were dressed like businessmen on vacation, in polo shirts and chinos. The taller one was thin and had a well-groomed goatee. The shorter one was stockier and his shaved head glistened in the sunlight. Expecting them to step into the parking lot, I was surprised when they turned the corner and headed toward a small building at the edge of the property.

"What's that?" I asked Remy.

"I have no idea."

"Well, then let's find out." I pulled out my cell phone, located my most recent incoming call, and hit the send button. Abigail Flowers picked up after the second ring.

"Mrs. Flowers?"

"Speaking."

"This is Deputy Murdock."

"Yes, dear. What can I do for you?"

"Taking your advice, I'm here keeping an eye on things, and I was wondering what was in the small building on the east side of the resort."

"That's our well house. Why do you ask?"

"Two men just exited the front door and are walking toward it."

"That's them! They asked where they might find Tom, and I suggested they try his room which is in the same building."

"I see. Thank you ma'am." I disconnected. "They're looking for…"

"Tom," Remy said, nodding toward the men who stood with their backs toward us.

"I wish they'd turn around so I could get a better look at them."

"Don't look like he's real happy to see those two."

I had to agree with Remy. Tom stood with his hands at his sides and his eyes shifted from one man to the other. As their heads bobbed and their hands gestured, it became clear they had a lot to discuss with him.

"Wonder what they're saying?" Remy said.

"If I had my binoculars, I might be able to tell you." I squinted through my sunglasses at the trio.

"Will these help?" Remy held out a pair of field glasses. They were huge and had to be older than I was. "I've had these since I was a young man, but they still do the trick."

I pushed my glasses up on my head and looked through the lenses. Tom's bronze face popped into view, and it looked paler that usual.

"Well, what's he saying?" Remy asked.

"Something about his partner being killed and…"

"Uh oh. Doesn't look like those two fellas liked that too much."

I lowered the binoculars and watched as the two out-of-towners became more animated, no longer taking turns. Tom took a step back with both hands raised. He began speaking, and I watched through the field glasses, hoping to make out a few more words.

"... have the stuff..." I relayed to Remy. "...need some time... get it... a few days." Then he stopped.

When I set the binoculars aside, I saw that his companions were doing all the talking again. Each time the taller one shook his head, Tom nodded in agreement. Then, without warning, the conversation ended and the two men turned to leave. Raising the binoculars one more time, I also recognized the pair from their pictures.

"To hell with Sandusky," I said, pulling out my cell phone again. Checking my watch, I was certain Sue was still in the office back in Virginia. I scrolled through my contacts for her number and initiated the call.

"Sue, it's Sarah," I began as soon as she answered. "I have a positive ID on the two men I emailed you about, and they are at my location right now. I have no idea how long they will be here, but it seems their contact here is setting up some kind of meeting."

"That's great! We've been after these two for a few years. I'm pretty sure I can have someone there in forty-eight hours. I did some checking and I see you have an airport in Cedarville. Is it large enough to accommodate a jet?"

"I think it could handle a small one, if it has a pilot who knows what he's doing."

"I'll get back to you with the exact time of arrival."

"Sounds good, Sue. Thanks." I hung up and watched as the men climbed into the Dodge and drove off.

"Well?"

"Someone should be coming; I just hope those two don't take off before they arrive."

"You want me to keep an eye on them for you?" Remy offered.

"That shouldn't be necessary. I'll call Abigail later and ask her how many nights they've booked the room. Why don't you take me back to my unit, and I'll finish up my patrol." I had almost a hundred seventy-five miles to cover before the end of my shift, but I didn't mind. I was in no hurry to get home and face the mess in my kitchen.

I said good-bye to Remy and got a large Mountain Dew from Sal. The sugar and caffeine helped for a while, but by the time I was driving through Cedarville later that afternoon, I could hardly keep my eyes open. That is until I passed the bar.

Certain I'd seen the primered fender of the little orange truck hidden behind the old building, I spun around and pulled in. I slipped out from behind the wheel and made my way down the brick wall. Peeking around the corner, I saw the vehicle was empty. I made a quick note of the license number and then went inside.

The interior was so dark I had to slide my sunglasses onto my head. Unlike my first visit to the Silver Spur Saloon, I was greeted by nods from most of the cliental, but because I was still on duty, I stepped to the end of the bar and motioned to Pete.

"Howdy, Sarah. Or is it still deputy?" he asked as he wiped the top of the bar with a towel.

"Still deputy." I leaned in closer. "I was hoping you could tell me who drives the small orange truck that's parked out back."

"Got primer on the back fender?"

"That'd be the one."

A big grin lit up Pete's face. "Belongs to your number one fan, Bill."

I scanned the crowd. "Is he here?"

"Should be. There was a phone call for him just a second ago. Maybe he's in the john."

I thanked Pete and went back outside. Looking down the side of the building, I wasn't surprised to find the truck gone. Anxious to end the day better than it had started, I got back in my rig, radioed the office to sign off, and drove home. Opening the front door, I was greeted by the lingering odor of scorched broccoli, which had intensified in the heat of the day. I changed into an oversized T-shirt and cutoffs and got started.

One by one I pulled the pots and pans out of the sink and filled it with hot soapy water. Then I grabbed the trashcan off the back porch and began dumping and scraping the remnants of the meal from hell into it. Two hours later I had most of the wreckage dealt with and had updated my evidence board with the pictures of the two men. Then I called Abigail at the resort; they were booked for two more days. After hanging up, I checked my email. A message from Sue confirmed that an agent from the Art Crime Team should arrive at the Cedarville Airport around ten o'clock day after tomorrow. A quick bite of something to eat, and I headed for the bathhouse.

Chapter 19

Floating in the hot water, I willed the tension to leave my body. No longer having to baby-sit Alexis, I hoped to focus on Gus' case and figure out just what was going on. And what about Bill? What that guy was up to was anybody's guess.

Looking through the small window of the bathhouse, I watched the large orange circle of moon climb over the ridge and up into the night sky. I was just about to slip beneath the water when Raven let out a horrifying sound that told me he was in trouble. The first thing that crossed my mind was the mountain lion. I flew out of the tub, struggled into my clothes, and took off for the house.

After grabbing a flashlight and my .38 Special out of the bedside stand, I stomped into my rubber boots and headed for Raven's pasture. As I got closer, I could see him at the bottom of the field, pacing back and forth and flaring his nostrils.

Just as I got halfway to the large horse, a vehicle fired up its motor and pulled away from a small, dilapidated shed on Remy's side of the fence. Blocked by a stand of willows, I didn't get a good look at it.

As I approached Raven, I whistled softly to let him know I was there. He responded but continued to move back and forth. Something still had him agitated. I stuck my gun into the front pocket of my cutoffs and switched on my flashlight. Not finding any injuries anywhere, I figured he'd eventually calm down, but when I turned to go back to the house, a loud crashing sound came from the old shed. Something or someone was still in there.

Drawing my weapon, I squeezed through the fence and crept up to the door. With my arms stretched in front of me and crossed at the wrists, I pushed the door open with my toe and stepped inside. Quickly I scanned the interior and was shocked when the beam from my flashlight passed over an elderly man seated on an old wooden crate. As he lifted his head I recognized him. "Remy!"

"Ain't you a sight for sore eyes!"

"What's going on?"

He rubbed the side of his head where ribbons of red flowed from a deep gash. "Caught a fella trespassing and he let me have it."

"Give me your handkerchief," I said, slipping my gun back into my pocket and sticking the flashlight under my left arm. I placed the blue and white material on his wound and applied pressure. "Can you walk, Remy? We need to get you back to the house and call an ambulance."

"Don't need no ambulance. Get me back to my place and I'll be just fine."

"But my house is closer." I lifted the blood-soaked bandana. "This cut is still bleeding badly."

"My ATV's up the hill a ways, parked in some bushes. I rode it down part way, then shut off the motor and coasted the rest of the way. Wanted to get the jump on the guy." He stood up slowly and swayed a bit. "Maybe I oughta lean on you a bit."

"Here, keep this tight against your head." I let go of the handkerchief and put my arm around his waist. "Do you know who attacked you?"

"Damn right I do. It was that good-for-nothing Bill. I caught him packing boxes out of my shed, and when I asked him what the hell he was doing, he hauled off and hit me."

"What was in the boxes?" I asked, as I guided Remy through the narrow doorway.

"How the hell should I know? Weren't my boxes. That reminds me..." He slipped out of my grasp and stumbled toward the back of the building. "Don't want to leave this behind," he said, grabbing a rifle that was leaning against the wall and cradling it in his left arm. "When I saw it was Bill, I figured I didn't need old Bessie here. Guess I figured wrong."

"Stay here for a minute." I made sure Remy had his balance, and then I went back to the front of the shed. Shining my flashlight in a wide arc, I found what I was looking for. Shoeprints, identical to those left behind by the mystery visitor to Gus' house, were visible in the soft dirt.

I hustled back to Remy. "Come on, we need to get you up the hill."

"You know that horse of yours saved my life."

"Because I found you?"

"No. That animal noticed me coming down the hill and followed me down the fence line. When Bill clobbered me, he made such a racket the guy took off. Otherwise I may have been done for."

"Here, you sit on the back and I'll drive." A few instructions from Remy, I fired up the bike and drove him back to his place.

After getting him settled in one of the kitchen chairs, I went in search of his first-aid kit and finally located it under the bathroom sink, clear in the back. It looked to be almost as old as his binoculars, but it was well stocked and I had his wound dressed in no time. "Are you sure you don't want me to take you to the hospital? You could have a concussion."

"Quit your fussing. Don't have no damn concussion. Good night's sleep and I'll be as right as rain."

"Well, if you're sure, I'll be on my way. I have an arrest to make in the morning."

"No sense you walking home. Take my ATV. I won't be needing it any time soon."

"Thanks, Remy. I'll come by in the morning and check on you."

"Appreciate that." He walked me to the door and I heard the deadbolt slide into place as I went down the front steps.

Back home, I wrote Bill's name on the photo of his shoeprint and fell into bed.

Chapter 20

When I knocked for a second time the next day and got no response, I started getting worried. I pounded on the door with my fist. "Remy!"

"Hold your horses." A voice came from far inside the house. "Can't a body go to the bathroom in peace?" There was more silence, and then I could hear the shuffling of feet approaching. The deadbolt slid back, and Remy opened the door. Huge bags hung below his eyes and the right side of his face was swollen.

"Wow, you look..."

"Yeah, I know and I feel just as bad as I look. Come on in." He let his hand drop from the doorknob, and he trundled to his chair. "My head feels like I drank a fifth of scotch, except I remember everything that happened, and I didn't get a buzz."

"You want me to fix you something to eat?" I offered.

"That's mighty nice of you, but I'm not too hungry at the moment."

"Well, you call me if you need anything." I pulled out one of my business cards and placed it on the table. "I'll let you know as soon as I have Bill in custody."

"I'd like that. Then I can put old Bessie here back in the closet." He nodded toward the door. Following his gaze I spotted his rifle leaning against the wall. "Just a precaution. In case that asshole comes back to finish the job."

"Take it easy today. I'll check on you again on my way

home." I let myself out and headed for Cedarville. I had no idea where Bill lived or who he worked for, but I did have his license plate number. At least I hoped it was his.

I radioed Cindy at dispatch, and she told me the vehicle was registered to a William Dunham, with an address on South Water Street in Lake City. I jotted down the number she gave me and signed off.

Fifteen minutes later, I'd located the residence but doubted it belonged to Bill. A sprawling ranch house surrounded by huge cottonwood trees sat at the end of the driveway. Numerous outbuildings, including a gigantic barn, were scattered about.

As I got out of my rig, the front door opened and a woman about ten years my senior stepped out. She wore a blue apron that posed the question "Where's the Beef?" over a pair of denim capris and flowered blouse. Her brown hair was pulled back and secured in a clip.

"Afternoon ma'am," I said as I approached. "I'm Deputy Murdock, and I'm looking for William Dunham."

"William? You must mean Bill."

"Does he drive a small orange pickup?"

"Sure does, but I'm afraid he's not here. He didn't show up for work this morning, and when Fred went to the bunkhouse, he wasn't there either."

"Fred?"

"Fred Fredrickson, my husband. Usually when Bill doesn't show up, it's because he's gotten drunk the night before. Fred just rouses him out of bed and puts him to work, but this morning there was no sign of him."

"Bill have any relatives in the area, or someone who might take him in?"

"No one I know of. He's not exactly a people person, you know."

"Yeah, I kind of gathered that." I handed her one of my cards. "Call me if you hear from him or he shows up."

"Sure thing."

I left Mrs. Fredrickson and headed on to Cedarville. Capturing Bill was going to be harder than I thought. Knowing old habits die hard, I decided to stop by the Silver Spur Saloon later in the day. For now, I needed to bring Sheriff Atkins up to speed on Gus' case. I stopped at the café and got a large coffee to go from Sal. Then I headed over the pass.

I found the sheriff in his office; unfortunately he wasn't alone. Undersheriff Sandusky was hovering over him, flipping through files and talking with the speed of an auctioneer. Judging by the look on Atkins' face, he'd have preferred the man had written him a memo instead.

"Murdock," the sheriff said when I peered around the doorjamb. "Just the person I wanted to see." Sandusky stopped mid-sentence and glared at me through squinted eyes. "Dirk, if you'll excuse us..." The undersheriff's face turned crimson as he began gathering up file folders. "You can leave those; I'll flip through them later." Enraged, the bureau-wanna-be stormed toward the door. "And close that behind you on the way out, would you?" the sheriff added. One more look of hatred directed at me, the second in command slammed the door with such force that it was several seconds before it stopped vibrating.

Sheriff Atkins rummaged around on his desk until he located a small piece of pink paper. "Who's this Sue James and why is the FBI calling me?"

"It doesn't say why on the memo?"

"Just says she called and asked me to call her back."

"Well, you see sir..." Mentally I crossed my fingers. "Sue is a former associate from the Federal Bureau of Investigation and the Program Director for the Art Crime Team. I'd contacted her in regards to known individuals on the west coast dealing with stolen artifacts. She was able to inform me about..."

"Never mind the 'official report' Sarah. I get enough of

that crap from Sandusky. Just fill me in, and we'll worry about proper protocol later."

I breathed a sigh of relief. "Yes, sir. Turns out there are several men the bureau is interested in, and she sent me their pictures. I showed them to people I questioned about Gus, and the owner of High Desert Hot Springs recognized two of them. Well, the next day they showed up at her place, so I called Sue and someone from her team should be here tomorrow."

"And you're certain they're the men in question?"

"Yes, sir. I saw them myself."

"Uh huh." The sheriff stared at the pink memo in his hand and drummed his fingers. "Okay. Here's how we're going to handle this." He layed his forearms on his desk, leaned forward, and looked me in the eye. "I want you to be our liaison with this guy from the FBI, and I want this whole thing kept low-key.

"Of course, sir." I got to my feet and started for the door.

"And Murdock..."

"Sir?"

"No more surprises."

"Yes, sir. I mean, no sir. That is — I'll keep you informed, sir."

"See that you do. Now get out of here; I've got work to do."

On my way out, I passed Sandusky standing in the doorway of the break room. His arms were folded across his chest, and he had a scowl on his face. Without even thinking, I flashed him my best smile. Seething with anger, he tromped back toward the sheriff's office.

As soon as I got back to Surprise Valley, I began an extensive search for Bill. After cruising each and every street in Cedarville, I traveled to the neighboring towns of Eagleville and Lake City, but there was no sign of him or his vehicle.

Back in Cedarville, I popped into Morrison's Mercantile for a microwaved burrito and to ask if anyone had seen my suspect. The stop was a waste of time; my lunch was still cold in the middle, and Bill hadn't been in the store for days.

Hoping I'd have better luck with Pete, I parked in front of the Silver Spur Saloon. The place appeared to be empty, but I could hear someone moving around in the backroom.

"Hey, Pete. How's it going?" I said as I stepped inside. The narrow room was lined on three sides with deep metal shelves that held cases of a variety of hard liquor and beer. A small metal desk covered with a mountain of paperwork was shoved against the fourth wall.

"Holy crap!" Pete almost dropped the box of empty beer bottles he was holding. "Don't scare me like that!"

"Sorry. Didn't mean to startle you. I've got a favor to ask."

"You betcha." He added the box to a stack in the corner. "Shoot."

"I'm still trying to locate Bill. I need to ask him a few questions, so if he shows up, will you give me a call?" I handed him one of my cards. *At this rate, I'll need a new box of these real soon.*

"Be happy to oblige." His blue eyes twinkled as he smiled at me. "Anything else I can do for you?"

"Not today, Pete. Thanks." I left him to his chore and climbed back into the Ford Explorer. Maybe I'd misjudged Bill. Maybe he'd already taken off, but my gut told me he was still somewhere in the valley.

Looking at my map of the area, I checked for places where the man might try to make himself disappear. Lake Annie and Fee Reservoir both had only one way in. If he were at either location, he would be trapped. And being on the north end of the valley, they were also close to home.

Reaching the turnoff to Lake Annie, I pulled onto a dirt road, which ran along a bare field before sharply turning to the left and winding through sagebrush. As I crested a small hill, the lake came into view. More like a gigantic pond, it sat part way up a rocky hillside at the base of a small knoll. The pungent smell of the knee-high sage filled the air. A white 1962 Chevy pickup was the only vehicle there, and its owner was fishing from an aluminum boat. I turned around, waved at the fisherman, and headed for Fee Reservoir.

It took longer to reach the reservoir than I expected; the washboard road shook the Explorer so hard I thought it was going to come apart. Created on a desert plateau, the large body of water had a surreal feel to it. Stunted juniper trees lined the edge, and large lizards lounged on sun-warmed boulders. The hot, still air was oppressing, and the hum of crickets vibrated in my ears. As I walked through the deserted campground looking for any signs of recent traffic, I knew this would be a perfect place for Raven and me to explore.

Back on paved road, I radioed dispatch and asked Cindy to put out an APB for William Dunham and his Toyota pickup on the chance he might be spotted before leaving the county. Then I headed to Remy's to tell him not to put Bessie away just yet.

Chapter 21

After a good night's sleep and a fresh pot of coffee, I felt more like myself. I'd checked on Remy and was glad to see he was feeling better. With a few hours to kill before meeting the incoming jet, I decided to patrol along the Nevada border. I was just turning west onto Highway 299 when my cell phone rang.

"Deputy Murdock."

"Deputy, it's Abigail Flowers again."

Panic seized my heart. "You aren't calling to tell me that your two guests have left, are you?"

"Well..." There was a long pause. "I'm not sure."

"What do you mean you're not sure?"

"I think they're missing."

"Missing?"

"Yes, dear. You see, I was out watering my prize roses yesterday morning — I think they're going to bring me best of show again this year at the county fair. They have a most unusual color in the center that seems to catch the judges' eyes..."

"Uh, Abigail?"

"Yes, dear?"

"What about the two men?"

"Oh yes, I'm sorry. Anyway, I was watering my roses and I saw the three of them..."

"Three of them?"

"Tom was with them. They pulled out about seven-thirty yesterday morning and haven't come back."

"Is it possible they're just on a road trip?"

"Well, I guess they could be except Tom was supposed to help my husband yesterday afternoon, and it's not like him to not show up like that."

"Yes, ma'am. Are they in the Dodge sedan?"

"That's right."

"I'll keep an eye out for them."

"Thank you, dear."

I disconnected and cursed my bad luck. Not only had Bill disappeared, so had all the probable suspects in the Gus Miller case. How much worse could it get?

After an uneventful patrol along the east side of the valley, I headed for the Cedarville Airport. On the way there, I rehearsed what I might possibly say to the agent without sounding like a complete idiot.

As I drove around the main office, I noticed several small aircraft, including a bi-plane, huddled around the hangar. On the other end of the field, partially hidden by a low, narrow shed, were a small plane and the brown Dodge sedan from the High Desert Hot Springs. Wherever the three men had gone, they were back.

I parked the Explorer in a secluded spot and got out. Not wanting to attract unwanted attention, I leaned against my unit and waited. Within a few minutes, I heard an approaching aircraft. After circling a couple of times, the tiny jet landed and began to taxi toward the far side of the airport. Hoping to maintain some element of surprise, I stepped forward and motioned for the pilot to park by the hangar instead. He obliged and pulled in next to the bi-plane.

The jet powered down, and two men climbed out. Dressed in a pair of tan cargo shorts and blue polo shirt, the pilot quickly began the task of securing the aircraft. The other man, wearing a dark suit and sunglasses, looked like an escapee from a *Men in Black* movie. He was either a rookie or a hard-ass.

"Deputy Murdock, I presume," he said, pumping my hand twice when he got close enough.

"That's right. And you are?"

The man removed his glasses, and I stifled a gasp. His eyes, much too large for his face, gave him a most freakish appearance. "Special Agent Michael Baxter of the Art Crime Team."

"How long have you been with that unit, Special Agent Baxter?"

"Oh please, call me Mick. You know, as in Dundee," he added, winking at me with one of those froglike eyes. "I've only been there for a couple months. While I was at the academy, there was an opening with the ACT and, since I've always had this thing for history and artifacts, I thought it was the perfect opportunity for me."

"And this is your first assignment?"

"Well, yes. How did you know that?"

"Oh, just call it a hunch. So what's the game plan?"

"Game plan?"

"Yes, how would you like to proceed?"

"Oh, that. Well, do we know the location of our suspects?"

I pointed toward the far end of the airfield. "That's the car they've been using from the resort, and I believe the plane belongs to them."

"Well then, shall we stroll over and pay them a visit?" He put his glasses back on and took a step.

"Hang on a second," I said, reaching out and taking hold of his arm. "Why don't we drive down there? My patrol unit is right here." I gestured toward the Explorer.

"Don't be silly. It's not far and my legs could use a good stretch."

"Trust me, we need to do this my way." I released my grip and started for my vehicle. All we needed was to give the guys in the plane time to panic as we made our way down the tarmac. My way, we wouldn't be such an easy target.

As we pulled up next to the resort's car, the lack of movement made me uneasy. Were they so involved in what they were doing that they hadn't seen us approach or was it some kind of trap? Special Agent Baxter didn't seem to share my concern as he popped out of the rig and practically ran to the door of the plane. Before I could get to him, he'd rapped on the side of it. As soon as I reached him, I pushed him to the side.

"What the..." he protested.

"Just stand over here until we determine what we're up against." *Sue's going to owe me for this.*

A minute or so passed and nothing happened; not one sound came from inside. "That's odd, don't you think?" the man said.

"Yeah, and so is this." I pointed to the door latch.

Agent Baxter pushed his glasses up on his forehead and leaned closer. "You know that looks like ..."

"Blood."

"Blood?" His eyes widened, giving him an even stranger look.

"We may have a problem."

"Blood?"

Good grief. "Wait here." I started back around the front of the plane.

"Shouldn't we call someone?" Agent Baxter asked as he followed me back to the Explorer. "I mean, if something's happened, don't we need to inform the proper authorities."

"Look, Baxter..." Hoping to calm the hysterical man standing at my shoulder, I tried another approach. "Mick, we have to determine whether or not there's been an incident first."

"An incident! There's blood on the side of that aircraft!"

"That's right and we need to determine how it got there." I opened up the back of my unit and grabbed a latex glove. "Now, let's take a look inside." Retracing our steps, we moved back around the plane. "Are you ready?"

"I guess so."

"Then you might want to draw your weapon and cover me," I said, pulling my own 9 mm out of its holster.

"Weapon? Oh yeah." The agent pushed his sunglasses down into place and retrieved a Glock from under his suit jacket. Then he gave me a thumbs-up.

Flattening myself against the side of the plane as best as I could, I reached for the door with my gloved hand. As soon as the latch released, I swung the door open and leaped into position.

"Omigod! I'm going to be sick!" Baxter, who had moved in close behind me, clamped his left hand over his mouth and ran for the clumps of sagebrush along the edge of the tarmac.

So much for my backup... but I could hardly blame him. I'd seen my share of gruesome murders, and this one easily ranked among the top five. Both men had multiple stab wounds and slit throats. There was blood everywhere and that distinct copper smell hung in the air. I was just about to radio dispatch and get some help when something caught my eye. At first I wasn't sure what it was, but by shifting my vantage point, I realized it was the small leather pouch I'd seen hanging from Tom Lowry's neck.

Leaving Baxter to get himself together, I returned to the Explorer and got on the radio. "Modoc, 113."

"Go ahead 113. This is Modoc."

I hesitated. The last thing I needed was a crowd of curious residents. "I need you to contact me on my cell."

"Copy that. Stand by."

Within seconds my phone rang. "What's up, Sarah?" Cindy asked.

"I've got a mess at the Cedarville Airport. I need a coroner's van to pick up two bodies. Could you also contact Deputy Jenkins and have him meet me here?"

"What is it, a vehicle accident?"

"I believe I'm looking at a double homicide." A

prolonged silence made me think I'd lost service. "Are you there, Cindy?"

"Yeah, sorry. I'm here. Wow! I'll get the meat wagon rolling and radio Scott."

"Thanks. Oh, and one more thing. Put out an APB for Tom Lowry, wanted for questioning." I hit the end button and then placed another call.

"High Desert Hot Springs."

"Mrs. Flowers, it's Deputy Murdock."

"Yes, dear. Have you found them?"

"Actually I was wondering if Tom had shown up by any chance."

"I haven't seen him return."

"Is it possible he could have come back without being seen?"

"Well, I suppose he might have. Do you want me to go out and check his room?"

"No ma'am, I don't. I don't want you to go anywhere near his place. I have to wrap up a few things where I am, and then I'd like to come take a look around."

"Certainly, dear. Whatever you say."

"Thanks Mrs. Flowers." I hung up and moved to the back of my unit. As I began pulling out the equipment I'd need, my phone rang. It was Scott. I brought him up to speed and asked if he would come take over so I could follow up on a lead. He gleefully agreed, and we disconnected.

By the time I got my gear to the plane, most of Special Agent Baxter's color had returned. "Feeling better?" I asked.

"A little. What now?"

"I need to start processing this scene. Up to helping me?"

"Uh, well... maybe."

"Relax. You can work on the car. Go through it and see if you can find any clues."

"The car?" His face brightened. "I can do that." He grabbed the latex gloves I was holding and disappeared around the plane. I didn't expect he'd find much, but it would keep him occupied.

I began taking pictures of the interior of the plane, watching for any kind of evidence. Beside the medicine bag, I found a small handgun with one fired round. Looking around I spotted where the bullet had embedded itself in the back wall of the cabin. I collected it as well as the gun and the leather pouch, and was just climbing down the small, narrow steps when Deputy Jenkins pulled up.

"Boy, you're a definite crime magnet aren't you, Sarah?" he said, strolling over to the plane.

"Put a sock in it, Scott. I need you to wait for the coroner and finish processing the scene. Here's what I found so far," I said, holding up the bagged evidence. "Get what fingerprints you can, too."

"So, who's inside?" he asked.

"Special Agent Baxter can fill you in. He's processing the car. I need to get going."

I threw my gear in the back of my patrol unit and headed for the resort. When I pulled into the parking lot, Mrs. Flowers was waiting for me on the front steps.

"Still no sign of him, dear," she called as I made my way across the parking lot. "Has something happened?" She began wringing her hands on the lower end of her apron.

"There was some trouble at the airport..."

"Is our Tom all right?"

"I'm not sure ma'am. That's why I'd like to locate him. May I look at Tom's room now?"

"Tom is awfully particular about who goes in there. He won't even let the maid or me change his sheets. You know how it is with bachelors. I always thought that if we took care of it, he wouldn't have to fret about it none..."

"Uh, Mrs. Flowers?"

"Yes, dear."

"May I see his room, please?"

"Oh, I'm sorry. I got carried away again. I guess it

would be all right." She pulled a ring of keys from her apron pocket. "I'll unlock the door for you."

"If you don't mind, I'd like to check it out by myself first. Which key is it?"

Abigail looked disappointed but flipped through the keys and held out a large gold one. "The lock is old and it sometimes sticks. Pull back on the knob and the key should turn."

"Thank you, ma'am. I'll bring these back to you when I'm done." I started toward the small building.

"Oh, I meant to ask you," Abigail called, "what about the two men?"

"That reminds me," I said, stopping and turning around. "I need you to do me a favor."

"Certainly, dear." Her smile brightened her whole face. "What can I do for you?"

"I need you to make sure no one goes into their room."

"Oh dear." Her face fell again. "The maid was in there yesterday, straightening up and putting out fresh towels."

"That's okay. Just make sure no one else goes in there until I get a chance to look at it."

"But what if those men come back?"

I walked over to her. "I don't think that'll be a problem."

"Oh my! You don't mean they're..."

I gave her a weak smile and once again started for Tom's room.

"Ed!" Mrs. Flowers called over her shoulder. "Ed, come here quick. You're not going to believe this."

I looked back and saw the short-statured woman practically running back to the entrance, probably anxious to seal off the room with makeshift crime tape of some kind.

After a couple of failed attempts, I managed to unlock the door and swing it open.

Chapter 22

The lack of windows made the small room dark and dreary, and the furniture didn't help much either. A twin bed with a sagging mattress took up most of the right-hand corner. The nightstand next to it looked vaguely familiar; a table and chair huddled next to that. A narrow counter ran along the left wall and around the corner toward the door. It held a rusty sink and propane cook top, and a small refrigerator sat on the floor underneath it. A crudely built set of shelves containing a few dishes and some food hung over the counter. Behind the door, a small television was perched on an old scarred dresser at the foot of the bed. All the comforts of home.

I flipped the light switch and a single, bare bulb hanging from the center of the ceiling blazed. The extra light provided no warmth and made the room seem even more austere. The only decoration in the place hung over the bed. It was a large ring with a woven design inside, and three black and white feathers dangled from the bottom.

Stepping across a threadbare, braided rug, I pulled open the drawer of the nightstand and looked inside. A black Bible with a picture stuck in between its pages and a hunting knife in a suede sheath were the only items in there. Opening the Bible, I examined the picture. A dark woman with long black hair stood next to an angry-looking young boy of about thirteen. On the back, written in a shaky hand, were the words 'Grandma Bertha' and

'Tom'. I replaced the photo and jotted down the name in my notebook.

After a thorough search, which revealed only a stack of out-dated Playboy magazines under the bed, a wardrobe of well-worn clothes, and some unidentifiable piece of food reclining on a plate in the fridge, I relocked the door and went in search of the proprietor.

"Mrs. Flowers," I called as I pushed through the front door.

"In here, dear." Her voice came from the right. Looking that direction, I spotted a room that I hadn't noticed on my previous visits. As I stepped through the doorway, it was like stepping into the nineteenth century.

"Wow, this is an extraordinary room," I said looking around. A round oak table with high back chairs sat in the center, and other unique pieces of furniture lined the walls.

"Isn't it wonderful?" Abigail was seated before the front window at what appeared to be a small drop-leaf desk. She jumped to her feet and moved in next to me. Taking my arm, she directed me to the right. "This trunk came west with Ed's family in a covered wagon. Well, actually it didn't quite make it all the way. After crossing the Nevada desert for many long, hot days, they had discarded it just before dropping down into Surprise Valley. They took a wagon back a few weeks later and retrieved it." Next she led me to the desk where she had been sitting. "I found this ladies' writing desk at one of those delightful estate sales. It was practically in pieces when I bought it, but given a little TLC, a thorough stripping and re-staining it looks good as new."

"Uh, Mrs. Flowers..."

"This upholstered rocker matches that lounging couch over there." She pointed across the room. "They belonged to my grandmother who lived back east, and when she died I had them shipped out here. I think they go perfectly, don't you."

"Please, Mrs. Flowers..."

"And this washstand," she said as we continued around the room, "was part of the bedroom set that Ed's grandparents had shipped here from San Francisco. We still use the bed but I thought this looked much better in the parlor. Now this box stove came from the old general store in Fort Bidwell. With the two burners on top, it comes in handy when the electricity goes out. Do you know what this is?" she asked pointing to the next piece of furniture. It was a large rectangular cabinet with intricate carvings and inlaid pieces, but there were no drawers or latches visible.

"Is it a phonograph of some kind?"

Abigail removed the large fern from the top and set it on the oak table. Then she pulled on the front right corner of the unusual cabinet, and it opened to reveal an antique sewing machine. Next she unfolded the top into a large flat surface that held whatever was being stitched. Last she reached down from the top and pulled the sewing machine up into place. "This is a genuine Burdick sewing machine. I found it at a local yard sale a few years ago."

"Yes, Mrs. Flowers this is all very interesting but..."

"I already mentioned this lounging couch and this," she said pointing at a small wooden box on legs, "is the commode that goes with the washstand." She giggled. "We didn't want to use that in our bedroom either. And this..." Finally we stood before the last piece of furniture, a bookcase that had each shelf enclosed behind a pane of glass. "This came out of the Surprise Valley Bank in Cedarville, which was in the brick building where the grocery store is now. There were three other sections but they were damaged so badly that..."

"Abigail!"

"Yes, dear."

"I don't mean to be rude but I really need to ask you about something and then continue with my investigation."

"Oh, of course. How can I help you?"

"Does Tom have anyone around here that might give him refuge?"

"Well, let me think. Both his parents were killed when he was a boy and for a while he lived with his grandmother on the reservation. What was her name?"

"Bertha?"

"Why yes, that's it. How do you know that?"

"I found a picture with that name written on the back. Do you know if she's still alive?"

"Yes, I think so. She lives on the reservation near Fort Bidwell."

"Thanks, Mrs. Flowers. You've been a great help."

Driving north toward Fort Bidwell took me back by the airport, so I decided to stop and see how Scott and Special Agent Baxter were doing. Pulling around the main building, I saw that the coroner's van had arrived, and Scott and another deputy were wrangling a body bag inside. I parked close and went around to the door of the plane. Baxter was at the edge of the tarmac inspecting the clumps of sagebrush again.

"Got a couple of good fingerprints off the door," Deputy Jenkins said when he joined me. "Didn't find much else though." He looked toward the FBI man dressed in black. "What's with him? I thought he was supposed to be a tough guy."

"Apparently not," I replied. "I think he's more of a scientist than a pistol-packing lawman. Hey Mick," I called. "I have another job that might suit you better." The man straightened up and gave me the thumbs-up. A few seconds later he made his way over to the two of us.

"I need you and Jenkins here to go over to the resort and search the room these two men were staying in. See if you can find anything to link them to dealing stolen artifacts."

"Will do," he said.

"We should be finished up in a few minutes," Scott said. "Then we'll head right over."

"Great. I need to make contact with someone over

at the reservation, and then I'll meet you back at the sheriff's office." I started back toward to the Explorer. "Oh, and Scott..." I spun around. "Be sure to tell Mrs. Flowers I sent you or she might not let you in the room." Then I got into my patrol unit and continued to drive north.

Chapter 23

Keep it low-key. That's what Sheriff Atkins had said to me. And no more surprises. Somehow I had a feeling that two dead suspects could be classified as a big surprise.

Tom's blood-spattered pouch linked him to the crime scene, and that made him my prime suspect. Hell, it made him my only suspect, but I had to find him first. I knew the grandmother at the reservation was a long shot, but I didn't have much more to go on. That is until I reached the huge alfalfa field by the turnoff to Lake City.

It took a moment for my brain to register what my eyes were seeing. At first glance, all I saw was a man walking across the green expanse. Probably a rancher checking on irrigation lines or animals, but there was no old pickup or ATV parked nearby. And this guy had a long black ponytail and was moving quickly. It had to be Tom Lowry.

I pulled over, dug out my binoculars, and made a positive ID. It was Tom all right, and it looked like he was headed for Gus' place. As soon as he reached the far end of the field and climbed through the fence, I eased back onto the road and turned left toward Lake City. Cresting a small hill, I saw him walk past Gus's house and enter the old decrepit barn fifty yards beyond it. *Now I've got him.*

I accelerated down the road and parked beside the old

house, positioning it between my vehicle and the barn. Then I got out and crept toward the big double door. I tugged open one of the massive panels and quickly stepped inside. Dust particles danced in the shafts of light coming through the dilapidated roof, which gave the interior an eerie feeling. Old wooden crates and broken furniture filled the stalls that lined the right side of the ancient building. Rusty farm equipment scattered about and a vehicle of some kind covered with a canvas tarp took up most of the other side. The man I was after had almost made it to the back of the building and seemed to be looking for something.

"Tom," I said in a loud clear voice as I advanced toward him.

Jumping like he'd been jabbed in the ribs, he whirled around. "What are you doing here?"

I placed my hand on the butt of my 9 mm. "You need to come with me."

"No, don't." His eyes widened, and he shook his head.

"Calm down." I extended my left arm, palm turned toward him. "I just need to ask you a few questions about the men in the plane."

He took a step toward me. "Wait!"

Then fireworks exploded inside my head and everything went black.

Voices — tinny and far away, like they're traveling through a long metal tube. My head throbbed, and my left arm tingled. As the voices grew louder, I realized my hands were tied behind my back and I was lying on my side.

"She never would have found me if it weren't for you. What'd you come here for anyway? All you had to do was lay low for a few days." The voice seemed familiar. Where had I heard it before? Barely opening one eye, I recognized the ragged jeans and tattered T-shirt, but this time they were splattered with blood.

"They're looking for me," Tom said.

"How the hell do you know that?" Bill asked. He stood next to his little orange pickup with his back to me. The tarp, which had hidden his vehicle so completely, was piled in a heap on the floor of the old barn.

"I heard her when she was talking on the radio."

"Where the hell were you that you heard that?"

"Hiding in the ditch. The guy in the suit practically puked all over me."

"What guy?"

"The one from the other plane — never mind." Tom rubbed a horizontal wound on his upper chest. "What'd you have to go and cut me for anyway?"

"You shouldn't have tried to stop me. Those bastards were going to stiff me — after all I went through to get the stuff out of Gus' house and keep it stashed. Nobody cuts me out!" Bill leaned closer to Tom. "Doesn't look like I got you too bad."

"I'll live, but that must've been when I lost my medicine bag, and she found it in the plane."

"Tough break — for you." Bill laughed.

"But you killed the guys who were going to buy the stuff. What are you going to do now?"

"One of them was kind enough to leave me this." Bill held up a small, black cell phone. "I bet I'll find somebody in here interested in making a deal."

"But they think I did it."

"Yeah, so?" Bill slipped the phone back into his front pants pocket.

"I'll tell the sheriff it was you that killed those guys." Tom moved closer.

"Go ahead. You think they're going to believe a desperate half-breed like you. They don't even know I was there."

Tom's fists clenched at his sides. "What makes you think I'm going to let you get out here alive?" he growled.

"This," Bill said, pulling a gun out of his waistband. I was pretty sure it had come from my holster.

"What about her?" Tom nodded in my direction.

"Just one more of your victims. Now get her on her feet."

As Tom approached me, I knew I had to do something, but I wasn't sure yet what it was going to be.

"Tom, you don't have to do this," I said, as he pulled me up off the floor.

"Oh yes he does, or I'll let him have it right now." Bill pointed the 9 mm at us. "Now, come get my knife and finish the job."

Tom's gaze moved from me to Bill. "I... I... I can't do that," he said, shaking his head.

"Just pretend she's one of those stupid rabbits you're always raising and cut her throat. Now!"

Tom swayed slightly and stumbled back toward Bill, but before he got close enough to reach out and take the knife, a loud explosion pierced the air. Bill let out a howl as his outstretched arm jerked, and the gun went flying. At first I thought the weapon had discharged, but when I realized I hadn't been shot, I took advantage of the situation.

I hit Bill with a running jump side kick. As soon as he landed face down on the ground, I practically stood on his neck, cutting off his air and immobilizing him. Before I could do anything else, the barn door burst open, and Remy rushed in.

"Don't move!" he shouted, aiming his rifle at Tom.

"Hang on, Remy. Take it easy." I struggled to keep my balance on top of Bill. "Cut me loose so I can get this guy secured."

"I'll do it," Tom said, bending over and picking up the large Buck knife that had fallen to the ground.

Remy moved closer and levered another cartridge into the barrel. "That's just fine, but don't you so much as breathe funny or this .45-70 will put a plate-sized hole in you."

Tom opened the knife and stepped behind me. For a split second, I expected to feel the pain of the steely blade but instead only felt the rope binding my hands go slack. Then the man snapped the knife shut and dropped it back on the ground.

Without moving my foot, I reached down and latched my handcuffs around Bill's wrists. "Remy, I think you can lower the weapon now," I said. "I don't think Tom is going to try anything."

"Don't you want to handcuff him or something?"

"That won't be necessary, will it Tom?" He shook his head. "Besides, I don't have another pair."

Leaving Bill prone on the ground, I rubbed my own wrists and wiggled my fingers in an effort to restore the circulation. "How did you find me anyway?"

Remy cradled Bessie in his left arm. "I was listening to the scanner, and when I heard them dispatch another deputy to the airport to assist you, I thought maybe you could use my help as well. But by the time I got there, they'd packed up and were heading somewhere else. That there deputy told me you were going to the reservation up by Bidwell. I tried to tell the man that I hadn't passed you, and then he says you probably stopped off someplace. That's when it hit me. Maybe you'd come back to Gus' place for some reason, so I headed over here. I found your rig, and while I was looking around, I heard voices coming from the barn. When I looked in, I saw Bill holding you at gunpoint. As soon as he moved away from you," he nodded at Tom, "I let that good-for-nothing have it."

"Well, I'm grateful that you did, Remy," I said, slapping him on the back. "Now, see if you can find my gun."

I went out to my unit and radioed Scott for some help. Grabbing my evidence case, I returned to the barn. While I collected Bill's Buck knife and the cell phone he'd taken from the jet, Remy stood guard. Then I inspected the elusive orange pickup with the primered fender and found the boxes of artifacts. I sealed each one and stacked them by the door. The only thing left to do was photograph the suspects.

I removed the digital camera from my case and walked over to where Remy had them seated on a couple bales of hay. I took pictures of Tom first and then moved on to Bill. That's when I noticed he was bleeding.

"Remy, can you grab the first aid kit out of the Explorer?"

"You hurt?"

"No, but Bill is."

"Damn right I'm hurt, you crazy bitch! Not that you give a shit about..."

Tom jumped to his feet and grabbed the front of Bill's T-shirt with one hand and his right ear with the other. "If you don't shut up, I'm going to rip this off," he hissed.

"Whoa there, big fella." Remy aimed his rifle at Tom. "Sit yourself back down."

"It's all right, Tom; I'll take it from here. Looks like he got nicked when you shot the gun out of his hand," I said to Remy, after inspecting Bill's hands.

"Yeah, so..."

"Remy!"

"Hold your horses, I'm getting it."

While Remy fetched the kit, I swabbed Bill's hands and scraped his fingernails for blood evidence, fairly certain he hadn't washed them since yesterday morning. "Tom, I need to swab your hands as well."

"But I didn't kill those men."

"Then this will prove it."

He held his hands out and I collected what I needed. Then I bandaged Bill's hand, and we moved the two men outside.

Chapter 24

"About time you got here, young fella," Remy said when Deputy Jenkins pulled up almost an hour later. "We need to get this here prisoner locked up."

"We?" Scott looked at me and raised one eyebrow. "Well, *we* were halfway up Cedar Pass when your call came through. What's going on?"

"What's going on? We caught the damn killer, that's what's going on," Remy boasted.

"No kidding. How did you manage that?" Scott asked me.

"Oh, I had lots of help. I need you to take Bill to the sheriff's office," I said, pointing to where he sat against a rotting fencepost. "Book him on suspicion of murder and assault. I've already read him his rights."

"You bet." Deputy Jenkins grabbed Bill by his arm. "Come on. Get on your feet."

Bill let out another howl. "Watch it. I've been shot, and I'm practically bleeding to death."

"Take it easy. It doesn't look that bad," Jenkins said, turning Bill around. The wound on his hand had soaked through the bandage, turning it bright red. Special Agent Baxter took one look and slipped around to the other side of the patrol car and began retching.

"What's with him?" Remy asked.

"Weak stomach," I answered, winking at Scott. "I've got some boxes inside the barn that I need to send with you as well."

"Sure thing, let's get them loaded."

With Bill secure in the back, Deputy Jenkins, accompanied by a very pale Special Agent Baxter, headed for Alturas again. Tom and I would be right behind them, but first I had to deal with my backup.

"Look, Remy," I began, "I'm very grateful for all your help."

"That's what partners are for."

Partners? "I can handle it from here, so why don't you go on home. Get some rest."

"Are you sure you don't need someone to keep an eye on him?" he asked, looking in Tom's direction.

"I think I can manage."

"Well, all right then. If you're sure."

"I'm sure."

Remy threw Tom one last narrow-eyed look of warning, made his way back to his vintage Toyota Land Cruiser, and sped away.

"Now what?" Tom asked as we walked over to the Explorer.

"We get your wound looked at, and then I take you to the office and get your statement."

"You're not arresting me?"

"For what, making a bad decision? You're the only witness to a double homicide." We climbed in and started the long drive over the mountain. "Whatever made you get involved with those two in the first place?" I asked after we'd ridden a while in silence.

"Revenge."

"Revenge? On who?"

"My people. Because I am of mixed race, my tribe shunned me. My grandmother was the only one that did not turn her back on me. She told me of the old ways, including the sacred places where our ancestors were buried. But..."

"But what?"

"When I saw their bones and those things they'd labored so hard to create, I knew I'd made a mistake."

"Well, like I told you before, all those items will be returned to the proper authorities. And I'll do what I can to get your medicine bag returned to you as well."

"Doesn't matter."

"Why not?"

"Having it taken from me makes it bad medicine."

"Maybe you can make a new one."

"Maybe."

When we reached Alturas, I took Tom by Modoc County General where they cleaned and bandaged his wound. By the time we got to the sheriff's office, Bill had been booked and processed. Special Agent Baxter was in Sheriff Atkins' office and Deputy Jenkins was in the break room, devouring something he'd gotten out of the vending machine.

"Tom, I need you to wait in here," I said leading him down the hallway. After getting him settled in one of the interrogation rooms, I went in search of someone to interview him. As I hurried around the corner, I bumped into Undersheriff Sandusky.

"Well, if it isn't Nancy Drew," he said, rubbing his arm where I'd collided with him. A strange smile formed on his long, narrow face.

"Sir?" He seemed taller than I remembered.

"You were damn lucky, Murdock!" His whole demeanor changed as he glared down at me. "This office has certain procedures that are to be followed by everyone — including you. Got that? You pull this crap again, and I'll personally come down on you so hard it'll make your head spin. Now get out of my face!" He shoved by me and tromped off in the direction of the locker room.

My jaw clenched and my hands tightened into fists. I was about to go another round with the garbage can in the ladies' room when Sheriff Atkins stepped out of his office, followed by Special Agent Baxter. "Thanks for your report, Baxter. Let me know if there's anything else you need. Murdock," he called, "see that this man gets back to Cedarville." Without another word, the sheriff went back inside his office and shut the door.

"Looks like you're feeling better," I said.

Agent Baxter's ears reddened. "Sorry about all that, but I have never been able to stand the sight of blood."

"Yeah, I could tell. Come on, I'll buy you a cup of coffee." I started down the hall toward the break room. "And as soon as Tom is finished, we'll head back to Surprise Valley."

"Sounds great," he said, giving me the thumbs-up.

Good grief.

I left him with Scott while I went to the dispatcher's desk to check the duty roster. "I need — Cindy, what are you still doing here? Wasn't your shift over at four?"

"Yeah, like I'm just going to head on home without getting all the details." She rolled her chair closer. "Start talking."

I explained what had happened after finding the bodies in the plane and that I needed someone to interview Tom.

"Not a problem," she said. "Are you sure you're all right?"

"I've got a good-sized lump on my head, otherwise I'm good."

"Great. What time I should meet you tomorrow night."

"Tomorrow night? What's tomorrow night?"

"When you're introducing me to the owner of the — what's the name of the bar?"

"The Silver Spur?"

"The owner of the Silver Spur."

"Fine. I'll meet you there around seven."

"Better make it six. Can't afford to waste any time."

I shook my head. "Six it is. I'll be waiting in the break room."

When I got there, Deputy Jenkins was explaining the finer points of vending machine dining to Agent Baxter. I stepped over to the coffee pot, poured myself a cup of viscous brown liquid, and sniffed it. "Thanks again for your help, Scott," I said as I dumped it down the drain.

"You bet. We were glad to get in on the action. Right, Mick?" He nudged the agent with his elbow.

"Uh, well I guess so. Parts of it were exciting, anyway." His sheepish grin reappeared.

"So, did you find anything useful in the dead guys' room?" I asked, taking a seat at the rectangular table.

"I'll say!" Baxter retrieved a large black briefcase from beside the small couch and laid it on the table in front of me. "Each of them had an overnight bag. Nothing remarkable there. Just a change of clothes, toiletries — that kind of thing. But this..." He flipped open the latches, "...this is a major find."

The stacks of hundred dollar bills caught my eye first. There had to be at least fifty thousand dollars in the case. Next to the stacks of bills was a small leather-bound notebook. Inside was a list of names and addresses ranging from California to Wyoming. Looked like twenty in all. An itinerary and map of the western United States were tucked into the file holder attached to the lid.

"Check this out," the agent said, opening the map and laying it on the table. "These red dots match up to each location on the list. My guess is they were going to each of these places, meeting their contacts, and purchasing artifacts." His started talking faster and his eyes bulged even further out of his head. "You know what this means, don't you?"

"You can go in as the dealers and make arrests?"

The smile melted from his face. "Yeah, that would be it."

"Ah Sarah, you spoiled it for him," Scott said, opening yet another vending machine delicacy. "You should have seen him when we found that stuff. I thought I was going to have to perform CPR on the guy. Show her the book, Mick. That's the best part. You're going to love this." He joined us at the table.

Baxter carefully removed the stacks of money and

piled them next to the case. Then he handed me the book that had been hidden underneath. *The Dummy's Guide to the Black Market* was its title and a small sign on the front cover declared it 'a must read.'

"You're kidding, right? I thought these guys were part of an established ring. What would they want with a book like this?"

"I think they were doing a little business on their own," Agent Baxter said, replacing the book and money. "Most of the looting has been taking place in Oregon and on a much larger scale."

"Have you made a positive identification on the two of them yet?"

"I should get confirmation by tomorrow afternoon." He closed the briefcase and set it down on the floor.

"Dirk the Jerk's driving them to Redding as we speak," Scott said, licking chocolate icing off his fingers.

No wonder Sandusky was so angry. "So where are you staying for the night?" I asked Baxter.

His eyes practically exploded out of his head. "I have no idea! And I totally forgot about Tony!"

"Who's Tony?" I asked.

"My pilot. All this happened so fast, I haven't had time to call him. What I am going to do?"

"Relax. I may have a solution for you." I pulled out my cell phone and hit the redial button. "Hi, Abigail. It's Deputy Murdock."

"Finally! Ed, it's the deputy." There was a click, and I knew there was someone else on another line. "Did you find Tom? Is he all right?"

"Yes to both questions. He's being interviewed right now, but I should have him home in just over an hour."

"Oh, thank goodness."

"I was wondering if you had any vacancies for tonight? I have an FBI agent and his pilot who need a room."

"For you dear, anything. Have they eaten dinner yet?"

"No ma'am, I don't believe so. There's just one

problem. The pilot is still over at the airport and needs to be picked up.

"You hear that, Ed?"

"Yes, Abby. I'm going." Another click and we were alone on the line.

"We'll have everything ready when you get here."

"Thanks. I appreciate it." I disconnected. "You're all set. Mr. Flowers is on his way to get Tony and dinner should be ready when you get there."

"Fantastic. I'll call him and let him know what's happening."

"Great. While you do that, I'll see what's taking so long."

Chapter 25

Peering through the tiny square window of the interview room door, I figured there was plenty of time to call Sue James and let her know what was happening with the investigation. Especially since Special Agent Baxter seem distracted at the moment.

I pushed through the front door and into the warmth of the afternoon sunlight, which felt good on my sore muscles. Checking my watch, I punched Sue's cell phone number into my own phone and waited.

"Hey, girlfriend," she said when she answered. "I was just thinking of you. How are you and Special Agent Baxter getting along?"

"Sending him here was a mean trick to pull on me, Sue."

"Why, whatever do you mean?"

"Oh come on, you know what I'm talking about."

She laughed. "Yeah, but it was his first assignment..."

"You think so?" I interjected.

"...and I knew he'd be in good hands workin' with you."

"Well, I don't know about that. He's lucky I didn't get him killed today."

"What are you talkin' about?"

I quickly explained what had happened from the time Agent Baxter arrived to the conversation I'd just had with him, including the briefcase and its contents.

"Omigod, Sarah. Are you all right?"

"A little sore in places and a nice lump on my head, but other than that, I'm fine. But it looks like your team's going to be busy, if Mick's plan gets approved."

"Oh great, another plan. So how much longer will he be there?"

"A couple of days, at most. Thanks, by the way, for your help on this."

"Anything for a friend, you know that. And speakin' of friends…" She paused. "I know you're probably not interested, but an unusual piece of information crossed my desk today."

"Oh?"

"They found Hensley's car."

"So?"

"Sarah, it was burned out. Nothin' left but the charred frame."

"Where?"

"West of Salt Lake City, out on the flats. But there's more."

"More?"

"They're pretty sure there was a body inside." I didn't know what to say. Was I sad? Not really. Was I glad? Maybe. "Sarah? You still there?"

"Yeah, I'm here. Are they sure it's Richard?"

"Not yet. The car was just spotted yesterday."

"Let me know what you find out."

"You betcha. I gotta go; the train's pulling into Brooke Station." And before I could say good-bye, Sue hung up.

As I turned to go back inside, I noticed a man across the street. Dressed in camo pants and a green army coat, he leaned against the block building, a ragged backpack at his feet. His hair was long, his beard scruffy. I was fairly certain he was a transient, someone who thumbed rides. And yet there was something familiar about him — the tilt of his head, the way he crossed one leg in front of the other. Was he someone from my past, maybe from a previous life…

WHOA! Reality check. I'm more tired than I thought.
Shaking my head, I reentered the Sheriff's Office to gather my passengers and head home.

The trip over Cedar Pass was strange, to say the least. Mick continuously tried to engage Tom in conversation but only got single-word answers grunted from the front seat. Finally he gave up, and we rode in silence.

The closer we got to the High Desert Hot Springs, the more Tom fidgeted in his seat. By the time we pulled into the parking lot, he had skulked down so far, he was practically sitting on the floor.

"Looks like you've got quite a welcoming committee," Mick said, nodding toward the entrance to the resort.

Abigail Flowers and a man I assumed was her husband, Ed, came rushing out of the door and over to the Explorer.

"Tom, we're so delighted to have you home," Abigail exclaimed, tugging open his door and pulling him out of the vehicle. She gave him a big hug, and then dried her eyes on the hem of her apron. The man stepped forward, gave Tom's hand a firm shake, and clapped him on the back.

Abigail turned to Mick. "You must be the FBI agent who helped bring our Tom back to us."

He glanced my way, and I nodded. "Yes, ma'am. Special Agent Baxter at your service, but you can call me Mick."

"Please to meet you, Mick." She pumped his hand several times. "I'm Abigail Flowers and this here's my husband, Ed. Come on in, dinner's almost ready." She turned to me. "You're welcome to join us, dear."

"Thank you, Mrs. Flowers but..."

"Please, call me Abigail."

"Yes, ma'am. Thank you, but I need to be getting home. It's been a long day."

"Of course, dear. But please come back again soon." Then she turned back to the others and herded them inside.

As I drove north on County Road 1 past Lake City and on toward Fort Bidwell, the shadow cast by the Warner Mountains crept further and further east. By the time I reached the turnoff to my place, most of the light had left the sky. Passing Remy's, I decided to stop by and thank him again for coming to my rescue.

Ballads sung by the Highway Men greeted me as I climbed the front steps, and Remy yanked the door open before I reached the top one. "What in tarnation took you so long? I was beginning to think you weren't ever coming home. Get on in here and have something to eat."

"Thanks, but I just stopped by to see how you were doing. How's the head?"

He reached up and touched the large gauze pad taped to the side of his head. "It's fine. Now, come on and have some supper."

"I really need to get going," I said, backing up.

"Have you eaten?"

"No, but..."

"Something wrong with my cooking?"

"Of course not. I just..."

"Then get on in here and take a load off. I'll just pull the meatloaf and baked taters out of the oven and..."

"Did you say meatloaf? And baked potatoes?"

"Sure did, with all the fixins."

My stomach growled, and my mouth watered. "Well, maybe just a quick bite." I followed Remy into the kitchen and sat at my usual place. He grabbed a beer out of the fridge and plopped it down in front of me. Then he opened the oven and pulled out the biggest meatloaf I've ever seen, followed by four gigantic baked potatoes.

"All right," he said as he joined me at the table. "I don't care if you talk with your mouth full or not, but I want to hear every last detail."

So I told him everything that had happened since he left Gus' house. It took three slabs of meatloaf covered with ketchup and two potatoes slathered with butter and sour cream to get through it all, but I made it. An hour later Remy was satisfied, and I was stuffed.

"I need to get going, Remy. Thanks for dinner and for saving my ass today," I said, pushing back from the table. "You'll have to come over to my house for dinner some time soon."

"You cook?"

"Uh, not really, but I do okay heating things that come in a box."

"Uh huh. Well, we'll see. Now you get on home and get some rest."

"I will. Good night." I turned toward the door and was surprised to see Bessie hanging on the wall next to the front door. "I thought you were going to put your rifle back in the closet."

"Didn't seem right somehow," Remy said. "She did such a good job today; I figured she deserved to hang in a place of honor. Besides, she's handier here for the next time I need to back you up."

I rolled my eyes. "Good night, Remy. I'll see you tomorrow."

"Good night, partner."

Good grief.

Coasting down my driveway, I was never so glad to see my own place. Raven, standing near the fence, whinnied when I slid out of the Explorer. "Hello boy, am I glad to see you," I said as I unlatched the gate and stepped inside his corral. I rubbed his huge, flat forehead while he nudged me with his long nose. "I've missed you." A soft nicker was his only reply. After giving him a hug around his enormous neck, I threw him a flake of hay and trudged up to the house. Unlocking the door, fatigue hit me like a bus; every inch of my body ached. All I wanted was a long soak and a few more beers.

I undressed as quickly as my stiff muscles would allow and slipped into my bathrobe. Then I raided the fridge for beer and slowly made my way to the bathhouse. As soon as I got there, I turned on the hose and the deliciously warm water began to fill the tub. Then I lined the beers along the edge and within reach.

While I waited for water level to rise, I attempted to empty my mind of the Miller case. When the water was deep enough, I finished off my first beer, slipped into the hot water, and sank to the bottom of the tub.

My new career as deputy sheriff certainly hadn't begun the way I thought it would, but it had to be a fluke. I mean, just how many investigations could crop up in a small ranching community in a remote corner of northeastern California anyway?

www.ingramcontent.com/pod-product-compliance
Lightning Source LLC
Chambersburg PA
CBHW031309280626
47169CB00017B/1087